Nanny Higgins
Time Traveller

Danny Higgins
Time Traveller

Jane Schaffer

Illustrated by
John Lightbourne and Geraldine Mitchell

Seven Arches
Publishing

Published in May 2009
By Seven Arches Publishing
27, Church Street, Nassington, Peterborough PE8 61QG
www.sevenarchespublishing.co.uk

A catalogue record for this book is available from the British Library

Cover design by John Bigwood and Alan McGlynn
Book Design by Alan McGlynn

Printed in Great Britain by Printondemand-worldwide.com

ISBN: 978-0-9556169-3-8

For Natassja and Natalie Fairbanks
who gave their granny the idea for this series.

CHAPTER 1

Museums are so...oo Boring

The day had started badly for Danny. First he had discovered that, once again, his mum had managed to wreck one of his best T-Shirts by putting it in the wrong wash. (I mean how hard is it to get something like washing right?) Then for some mysterious reason he couldn't find his mobile. Finally, and by far the worst, he had found out at breakfast, that his mum and dad were planning a day out. Nobody, of course, had consulted him, he just heard them talking as they stood with their cups of coffee in the corner of the kitchen where they always lurked. From phrases such as 'Manchester's only forty minutes drive' and 'I'll put a few sandwiches together,' he knew his fate was sealed.

Danny stomped up to his room and continued his search for his mobile. He was not an untidy child, he was, in fact the opposite. His room nearly always looked like one of those rooms after a 'Clear out your Junk' programme on TV, completely uncluttered, neat rows of stationery items on his desk, books on the

bookshelf ordered by size, computer keyboard slid out of sight and all his clothes put away in drawers or cupboards.

Where could his precious mobile have got to? He pulled open drawers he had already looked in and peered under the bed again. Then he went down the corridor to Jenny's room to see if she had taken it, not that that was likely; his sister didn't do things like that but he thought it worth a try. Jenny's room couldn't be more different from his.

"I don't know how you can live in this mess," he said.

Jenny looked up and smiled at him. "It's my mess, Danny and anyway I'm going to clear it up today."

"Oh no, you're not," he said.

"Why not?"

"Cos Mum and Dad are planning a day out."

"Oh good. Where?" Danny had known that he couldn't expect support from Jenny in his intended revolt. His sister was one of those kids you just could not make cross. Danny wondered if she had been given a happiness pill at birth. Even when he insulted her in the worst way he could think of, she only got mildly upset. All through her babyhood she had just gurgled and smiled and Mum and Dad kept on saying 'not like Danny' which had made him think he must have been some freak baby who spent the whole day screaming.

"Jenny, it's a lovely day: the sun is shining. We haven't had a Saturday without rain for weeks – I could be out playing football with Mark and Griff. You could be playing in Bethany's play house – you know how much you like that." He paused to see if his words were having an effect, but Jenny's face showed no signs of changing from happy to sulky. "I wouldn't mind if we were going anywhere decent, but we won't be – we'll be going to that rubbish museum in Manchester, where we've been loads of times before."

Jenny just said, "probably," and carried on searching for some socks, which is what she had been doing before Danny came in.

Danny sighed and was about to go when he remembered what he had come for. "Oh, I don't suppose you have seen my mobile anywhere?"

"No, I haven't; have you lost it?"

"Yup."

"Danny, you never, ever lose things." Jenny looked up at him in complete incomprehension. "I just can't believe it. You must be having a bad day."

"I am," he said.

On the drive to the museum, Danny sat in the back of the car and pondered on the injustices of his life. For instance, today: any normal parent could see that an eleven-year-old boy, soon to be twelve, would not be thrilled at visiting a museum that he had already been to twice before. Especially not on a Saturday, a sunny Saturday, a Saturday made for playing football. But then neither of his parents understood football at all, or any other sport for that matter.

Why couldn't he have had a dad with a normal job? Like a policeman or an accountant or even a teacher? Who has an historian for a dad? His dad spent his days cataloguing boring old unintelligible papers at the university. Who would want to do that for a job? Mark was the luckiest boy ever. His dad had his own business and when the week-end came he didn't bother spending 'quality' time with Mark; all Mark's dad wanted to do was go off and play golf. The only time Mark saw much of his dad was when they went on one of their expensive holidays to amazing places like the Seychelles or Mexico. They had pots of money. Mark always had the latest computer. (Not for him the second-hand, clunky old thing that Danny had to nurse tenderly). Then, unfortunately, his mind wondered to Mark's phone, which was state of the art, and this made him remember the disastrous disappearance of his own.

He had mentioned the loss to Mum and Dad, not because he really thought that would make any difference, but just because he was getting desperate. Mum had made a sort of a search of the lounge on his behalf. But as she was completely hopeless at finding anything, even her own handbag or keys, he didn't expect a result. Besides, he had looked in there himself, and in every other room in the house. The thing was, he knew he had left it where he always left it – on the bookshelf in his bedroom beside the elephant-shaped money-box that he didn't use, but couldn't throw away because it had been a present from Gran.

When they got to the museum, Mum and Dad told them that they had come because the place had had a re-vamp; all the exhibits had been changed, made more 'interactive', whatever that meant. They went on about how this was happening across the country with museums and how it was all going to make it much more interesting and exciting for children. As if...Danny had thought.

Once inside though, he had had to admit that it was a big improvement on last time. For a start the

place was bright and airy, not the gloomy dark place he remembered. His mum and dad got so excited about the renovations that Danny decided he would really make an effort. As the family started out on their carefully planned route, from ground floor to third floor, he tried to look as enthusiastic as possible. He even managed a few questions. But it wasn't long before his usual boredom set in. As ever, he started staring blankly into space instead of at some oddly-shaped pot that had amazingly survived for over a thousand years and which was now claiming the undivided attention of both his mother and father, not to mention his sister.

Jenny, whose main aim was to draw everything she saw, was never bored. She eagerly pounced on the pads of paper and pots of pencils that were strategically placed in every room by this child-friendly museum. She left a trail of pictures for others to enjoy. Jenny is so good at drawing everyone said. No wonder thought Danny, she's had so much practice. Today Jenny had made a passable attempt at a dinosaur jaw bone, an ancient Egyptian mummy, three different types of pot and a pygmy's spear. She always captured a little point of detail that particularly impressed either Mum or Dad or, as happened in the Egyptian room, one of the museum staff. The museum lady said that she had never seen such good observational drawing, and had flapped around Jenny like a pterodactyl about to make a kill. She swooped on Jenny's finished drawing and carried it off with cries of: "oh we must have that for our central display board."

After this, his mother came across and said, "you see Danny, careful observation is what history is all about. Even the smallest detail can tell an amazing story."

"Mmm, Mum, I know it can," he replied. His mother gave a little sigh and then said, "we're off to the amphibian room now."

Danny perked up. Something living at last. He could never quite understand why there was an amphibian room in a museum. Surely snakes and frogs and things belonged in a zoo not a museum? And he always felt a little bit sorry for them, as if being in a museum made them more dead than alive. But he was not about to complain. He liked amphibians, especially frogs. When they reached the room with its huge tanks that gave the place the mysterious atmosphere of a green under-water world, he went round with Jenny explaining the parts of the labels that she found difficult to read. She was a good reader for a seven-year-old, but Danny was glad that there were still words like 'iguana' that she found difficult. It gave him the chance to be the older, wiser brother. The parents didn't follow them, but stood back with the looks of happy satisfaction that they always had whenever he did the 'older brother' thing.

After the amphibian room they made their way downstairs. Danny waited with anticipation for his mother to discover what he had realised some time ago. Although his mother had certainly made the sandwiches, and wrapped them all up in several recycled food bags, she had in fact forgotten to put them in anybody's rucksack. According to his calculations, they were still sitting on the kitchen table. They all four had rucksacks, just as they always did when they went on an outing; the sandwiches should, of course, have gone into one of the parents' rucksacks. Why neither of them had not sussed out that their bags were too light to be holding the lunch for a family of four he would never know. Anyway there was a good old rummage around in all of the bags at the bottom of the stairs and then a very flustered Mum apologising to everyone and saying that there was only some digestive biscuits, an apple each and two oranges for lunch. At which point, Dad managed to bite the bullet and say as cheer-

fully as he could:

"Well it will be a jolly good opportunity to see what the lunch is like in the cafeteria." The café was bright,cheerful and crowded. Danny and Jenny were sent to find a table, while the parents went to the counter to buy some food.

"I'm really hungry," said Jenny.

"Starving," Danny agreed. "I wonder what they'll get."

"I hope it's chips."

Jenny got her choice. The parents came back with four plates of sausages and chips and four drinks of orange juice in the little oblong-shaped cartons (the cheapest drinks available). They always got the same for everyone, no enquiring into anyone's preferences. Still sausage and chips wasn't bad and Danny started to tuck in happily. Mum and Dad kept apologising that it was not a healthy option, while he and Jenny exchanged conspiratorial glances that meant they were glad it wasn't. Then something strange happened. At least, it seemed strange to Danny – a waitress clearing plates squeezed past their table and the next thing he knew his plate with his lunch on it was upside down on the floor.

"I am so sorry!" the waitress exclaimed, turning

round. She was sure that she had caused the fall, but Danny was almost certain she had only brushed the side of the table. His plate had just seemed to bounce up in the air and descend to the floor all on its own. The woman rushed and got a broom and then insisted that Danny should go up and be given another plate of sausage and chips. Unfortunately, by this time, quite a queue had formed at the counter and Danny had to wait his turn for his replacement meal. When he got back to his family, they had all finished. His dad looked at his watch, his mother fiddled with her hair and Jenny said:

"I'd really like to do another drawing of the dinosaur bones."

"Don't be impatient Jenny, we've got to wait for Danny," his mother remonstrated.

"Oh no, don't wait. I'll be fine: you can go along without me... oops these chips are hot." Danny waved a hand in front of his mouth. "I'll be a while yet."

"Course Danny will be all right on his own. He's a big chap now." His father smiled at him and stood up, happy to get away. He had never liked cafes. "You'll find us OK won't you old chap? We'll be on the ground floor – dinosaur land."

CHAPTER 2

You Can Meet Some Weird People In Museums

Danny wondered why he was so happy to see his family go, after all he was very fond of them. He supposed it must be that even the relatively uninspiring sight of lots of humans scoffing food, was more interesting than looking round at a lot of dusty old things from the past, however well they were presented. The waitress clearing tables who had been involved in the upturned plate incident, came up and spoke to him again.

"It was nice of your family not to make a fuss," she said.

"Oh, it was an accident. It wasn't your fault."

"I've bought you an ice cream to say thank you. You do like them don't you?" She had an ice cream in a little glass dish which she put down in front of him.

"Oh yes, very much. You really didn't need to, but thank you."

After she left, a tall thin, boy of about twelve or thirteen slid into the seat opposite him. Danny made certain not to make eye contact but the boy kept looking at him intently and then said.

"Hello."

Danny speared a chip with great determination and pretended not to hear.

"Do you mind me sitting here?" the boy asked and Danny wanted to say 'yes' but didn't. Why, when the day had just started to improve one hundred per cent did some peculiar boy have to come and spoil things? He was probably going to try to get friendly and then see what he could get from him. Well, if he was hoping to steal a mobile he was out of luck.

"My parents are here at the museum and, for your information, I don't have a mobile on me."

"I know."

At this, Danny looked up at the boy and, for the first time, noticed his appearance. He was not very tall, about the same height as Danny but he looked much older. For some reason that he couldn't explain, Danny started staring at this boy, something he would never normally do. Very strange. Then the boy said something that was definitely strange:

"I've had to come to return something that belongs to you."

"What are you talking about?" Danny asked.

He was beginning to feel rattled. If he hadn't had at least five chips left to eat and the ice-cream, he would have left. For a moment the boy didn't say anything and then he took a phone out of his pocket and laid it down gently on the table in front of him. Danny looked at it; it was exactly like his. The boy slid it across the table towards him.

"It's yours – go on, have a look: you'll find all your numbers in it."

"It…. it can't be mine." Danny started to feel the hairs on the back of his neck stand on end. In the bright light of the museum café with dozens of kids and mums and dads eating snacks and slurping drinks, he was feeling afraid. As if hypnotised, he reached out and picked up the phone. Even before he checked his contacts he knew it was his.

"How did you get it?"

"I'll tell you the answer to that Danny, if you stop worrying and just try to like me a little. I'm not used to being disliked."

Oh my goodness, the odd boy knew his name! Danny fought back the urge to ask him to explain how he knew he was called Danny. But instead he just said gruffly:

"I'm not used to talking to strangers."

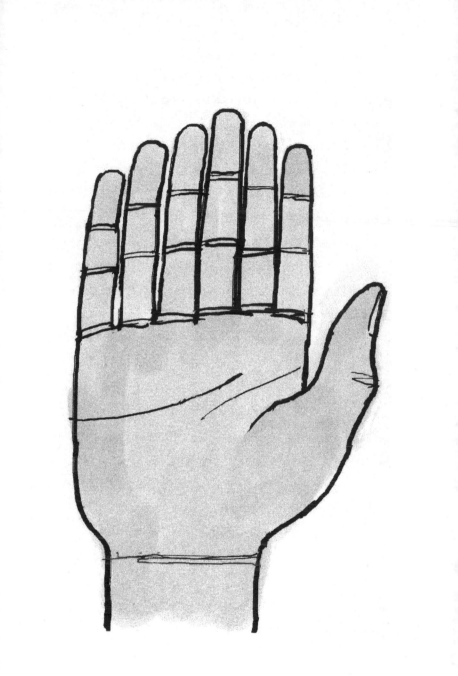

"Very sensible too, but I'm not a proper stranger. You see, I'm an alien, well sort of. I belong to a different time zone so I think that makes me an alien. Aliens are so rare you've got to talk to them." The boy was laughing now, teasing him, Danny thought, with this fantastical story. Then the boy held up his right hand and turned the palm towards Danny. Clear as day Danny could see seven fingers on his hand. Seven fingers on a hand that looked perfectly formed, not disfigured or anything, just a hand with seven long, thin fingers.

"You see, I'm quite different to anyone in this room – I'm from the future." Now he was really laughing, chuckling as if what he was saying was the greatest of jokes. His laughter must have been catching because Danny found himself laughing as well. An incredible thought flashed through his mind, maybe this boy is what he says he is – someone from the future. But no! Surely he must be playing some kind of a trick?

"I'm not sure I can believe you." Danny said, still chortling as if sharing a joke with a friend. "You certainly are strange and I certainly am glad to get my phone back, although come to think of it, I should be mad at you. Did you get into my bedroom somehow?"

"Nope"

"Well have you got magic powers or something?"

"They'll seem like magic powers to you but really it's just science to us. But Danny, I do have some really important things to say to you." All of a sudden the boy had become quite serious, almost worried. He leaned forward as if to convey a sense of urgency.

"I haven't got too much time, you see, much as I love being here. But time travel is dreadfully expensive and my dad has paid for this trip so that I can get experience for my out-of-time science degree. I've got to make you understand that what I'm saying is true. Perhaps this'll convince you. Watch the table over there." The boy nodded to a nearby table with a family of four. The mother got up and just as she did, a plate fell on the floor scattering the remains of her half-eaten lunch. Even though she clearly didn't cause it to happen, she obviously thought it was her fault.

"The sausages and chips? That was you?"

The boy nodded.

"No way!" Danny was stunned for a moment. "But why?"

"Because I wanted to talk to you without your very nice parents hanging about."

"I see. But why? And why did you take my mobile?" Hundreds of questions were crowding into Danny's mind. He had stopped eating his chips and the ice cream was melting.

"We had to take your phone because we needed to programme something in. Look on the front on the right-hand side."

"Oh my goodness! There are three extra buttons!"

"Exactly. Now listen carefully, Danny, as I said: I haven't too much time. The black button is for information. When you are alone, preferably at home, press the black button and you will be told all about SHARP 15798 – I must explain what SHARP stands for; it's the Scientific History and Art Reclamation Programme, and you're on the fifteen thousand, seven hundred and ninety-eighth programme." He said the last bit really quickly, the way people do when they're repeating a number that they've said many times before. But Danny was good with numbers.

The boy paused. Danny felt that he should give some sort of response so he nodded and said: "SHARP one five seven nine eight."

"That's right. I knew you would catch on fast Danny, that's why I chose you."

He's given me a compliment, thought Danny,

but he didn't say anything.

"The background to SHARP is that, with the start of the New Democracy, which replaced the Dark Chaos of the intervening years, humankind (that's everyone left on earth now – no nationalities just humankind) has been trying to piece together our history from the earliest of times. Unfortunately, so few records are left that we have to do it by time travel exploration. We mainly visit the twenty-first century which is sort of our limit. That is why we want you to travel back further in time and gather information for us."

"What?" Danny sat bolt upright as if given an electric shock. Surely he hadn't heard that bit correctly?

"As I said, the black button will explain everything. The green button will take you back in time and the red button is to return home. To make sure that you do not press either of those in error, you have to dial the 15798 project numbers first. It's very easy."

"Oh yes, very easy." Danny could see that the boy didn't realize he was being sarcastic.

"My name's Kazaresh, by the way. "And I'm your contact person on this project. All the messages you get will be from me, well most of them anyway. I have got my professor overseeing what I do, a Professor Aurelia Dobbs. She might contact you." He stood up as if to go.

"But you can't go yet." Danny jumped up and looked at him desperately. "I've got a whole load of questions – I just can't believe what I've been hearing."

"The answers are all there on your phone. And I have to go. I've got no choice, much as I would love to stay." He smiled, almost teasing. "I was hanging around for quite a while waiting for you. You should have been at the museum at least a half hour earlier – your dad is a very slow driver. How was I to know he is way below the average speed for drivers in this century? It used up so much of my time, and then the looking for the sandwiches. I couldn't believe it took them so long to get to the cafe."

"Tell me about it," sighed Danny. He wanted to ask if the boy had somehow been involved in the sandwiches getting left behind but he could see that it was now really important for him to leave. A very strange expression had come over his face and he was beginning to get blurry around the edges.

Kazaresh held out his hand to say goodbye. Danny hesitated for a moment. He wasn't sure he wanted to touch a seven-fingered hand. But then he stood up and shook the offered hand. (It didn't feel any different to a five-fingered hand except that it was cold, very cold).

"Goodbye Danny. I hope we get to work together."

"Goodbye Kazar...esh", Danny stumbled a little over the unusual name. "I really wish we could have talked longer, and I'm sorry I was so unfriendly at first."

"No sweat Danny. Oh and by the way, my friends call me Kaz." Within two seconds the strange boy was out through the café doors. Gone. Danny sat back down at the table. He stared at his mobile for several minutes, and then slipped it into his pocket and went off to find his family.

CHAPTER 3

A Full Explanation Of The Scientific History And Arts Reclamation Programme

They didn't get home until late because, instead of driving straight back, Mum had said she wanted them to have a 'quick look' at some Elizabethan manor house, a place called Bramall Hall. It was just south of Manchester and not that far off the motorway, but with the parents' poor map-reading skills (well they weren't too bad at it really but why couldn't they have SAT-NAV like other people?) it had managed to add well over an hour to their return journey.

It was closed when they got there, but all the same they got out of the car and walked up to have a look at the house, as the park was still open. Dog-walkers and parents with children who had been to feed the ducks, on the small lake below the house, were still wandering around.

In the usual way of things, Danny might have agreed that it would be a good place to visit, as the park nearby even had climbing stuff for kids of his age and, in any case, he always thought manor houses, castles and the like were preferable to museums. Today, though, all he wanted to do was to get back home to the privacy of his room. The mobile seemed to be burning a hole in his pocket. He was dying to have a quick look at it, so, as they got out of the car, he took it out of his pocket. Of course, he had to be spotted by someone didn't he?

"Oh, you've found your mobile, have you?" Dad said loudly. At this, Jenny and Mum clamoured to know where he had found it.

"You didn't find it in the car did you?" Jenny queried and then she added, a little accusingly, "you didn't say anything."

"It was in the inside pocket of my rucksack," Danny lied. "I found it just now. Wasn't that strange?"

"Yes, very strange." Jenny gave him one of her knowing looks.

"Well I am jolly glad it's turned up," Dad said. "I know it's like your right arm to you. What are you doing, sending a message to Mark?"

"Yup, I was just going to tell him we're on the way home but I won't see him till tomorrow." Danny fibbed some more.

His dad put his hand on his shoulder. "Oh I don't

know about that, Danny. I know you'd have liked to have seen him today." Dad was trying to make it up to him for dragging him off to the museum. "You could ask him round for the evening."

"No it's fine really – I've got some homework to finish off anyway." The last thing Danny wanted was Mark round. Danny was not going to say anything about the museum meeting to anyone, not even Mark, at least until he had checked out his phone. Fortunately, at this point, they reached the courtyard of the old house and his parents' attention immediately switched to the fine exterior of the building.

"What a wonderful example of a Black and White Cheshire Elizabethan mansion," enthused his mum. "We must come back soon for a visit." She walked over to a small notice board and jotted down the opening times.

Dad then started on about how, over the centuries, there had been various changes, additions and restoration to the structure, and that you could tell this by the different materials used. Then he got very excited. He pointed up at a window on the upper elevation.

"Look kids, at that wonderful carving!" Under a small curved window on the first floor, blackened

wood had been intricately carved into very strange fig-
ures. There was a dumpy little person, possibly an
angel, holding what looked like a shield, standing on
the head of a man. This peculiar head had branches
with leaves coming out of its mouth.

"That could be a depiction of the Green Man, a
mediaeval character who was supposed to herald the
start of spring," Dad said. "It makes this side of the
house the oldest part, I shouldn't wonder." Mum and
Dad stood discussing the carving while Jenny and
Danny scooted off round the side of the building letting off steam before they all piled back in the car for
the journey home.

Once safely inside his bedroom, Danny sat on the
floor, in the space between his bed and the radiator.
He took out piles of school books and scattered them
in front of him so that should he be interrupted, his
cover-up about doing homework would not be blown.
He didn't need to do homework; he always did it as
soon as it was set, so there was no way he was going to
be doing it on a Saturday night. It was amazing how
little his parents knew about him, but for once he was
glad about that. He sat looking down at his phone for
a few minutes. Then he pressed the black button.

Nothing happened. As he watched the black screen, he could feel his heart beating; thumping in a strange loud way inside his chest. Anticipation (or was it fear?) was making his hand shake slightly.

And then…oh my goodness! Oh no!…the phone seemed almost to come alive – the screen was expanding, sliding away from the base and hovering about an inch or two in front. It was at least 24 inches wide, the edges defined by a small black rim. A message was appearing in black letters on the background of swirling colours.

<Welcome Danny TO SHARP 15798>

You can put the mobile down now. The screen will stay in place until you press the black button again.

Danny gingerly placed the mobile on the floor beside him, never taking his eyes off the floating screen. The message faded. Danny watched as the background of swirling colours, more intense than any thing he had seen before, seemed to spin off the screen into the air around him. Then the screen cleared for a moment and the following text appeared.

This is an invitation to you to join our project. Thank you for taking the time to find out about us, and if you decide not to accept our invitation, we apologise for any inconvenience to you that might have been caused by the changes to your mobile phone. We will return it to its original state. We have contacted you because we think you are particularly suited to project 15798 but we will quite understand if you decline to take part. Your safety is of the utmost importance to us and in almost all respects we can guarantee that you can travel backwards in time and return to your home time zone without any ill effects whatsoever or any danger to yourself or the people you meet on your travels. However, every activity in life can result in danger, as I am sure you are aware, and so we cannot guarantee ultimate safety.

As soon as Danny finished reading, the screen faded and the next message appeared.

After you have read all the following, think about what we are asking you to do. All the instructions and communications after this come to you from Kazaresh, a fully-endorsed student of the university belonging to SHARP. Kazaresh's tutor, Professor Aurelia Dobbs may also contact you from time to time.

Finally, we want you to know that your involvement with this project is very helpful to us, the remaining humankind of the world, and that, although it will be impossible for you to understand why, you will be making a contribution to the continuance of civilisation upon earth.

Our Company Policy is: Be of good hope and travel back in time and return in the spirit of greater good for all humankind.

The screen changed once more. This time there was a countdown with numbers flashing past the screen so quickly it was impossible to read them until they began to slow, and then Danny realised it was a countdown of years. At 2008 the numbers halted and the following words appeared on the screen:

<INSTRUCTIONS to Danny Higgins from Kazaresh

Porterman>

Hello Danny. It was great meeting you at the museum. The instructions below come from me but they are standard SHARP instructions. You can ask questions by sending a text to SHARP 15798

<Pre-Travel Information>
When there is the possibility of a journey to a different time zone, the screen of your mobile will glow blue and you will feel a low-level vibration, different in pulse to its usual one. This may last for up to two hours your time. After that the opportunity will have passed BUT do not be impatient. If it is not possible to take up the opportunity there will be another one, they come along about every two or three days. You must fit travel around your normal life.

<Travel Information>
If you are ready to travel, make sure you are alone and somewhere where you will not be interrupted. You will be gone for between four to six minutes, your time. It will seem to you, when

you are on a time journey, that you are away for much longer. It is not desirable for anyone to see you go or return. So make sure that no one is likely to be worried by your disappearance or will be looking for you.

Wearing clothes is not helpful so you will need to strip down to just underpants. You will have received from us a small bag that you must wear flush to your skin. It doesn't need ties or anything. When you have taken your clothes off, press the bag to your waist just above your underpants and it will stay there. Do this BEFORE you press the green button to go. The bag contains a small silver disc that you must put on your forehead when you arrive. The disc is almost weightless so you will not notice it but it will record everything you see. It only activates when it is worn, and it only lasts a short while, so do not put it on until AFTER you arrive in the past. On your arrival, take the disc out and press it to your forehead. The backing disc will come away. Put this and your phone into the bag and secure the fastening. You'll find that the bag attaches itself to your skin without any dis-

comfort. It cannot be taken from you and as-
sures your safe return. I was wearing one in the
museum when we talked.

<Journey>

When you are ready to go, key in the project
number 15798 and press the black button. A
screen will appear that will tell you where you are
going, what you will see and who you will meet.
It identifies a Destination. This is not necessar-
ily where you land but the place that SHARP has
planned for you to visit. Read these travel instructions very carefully and when you are sure
you have understood them, key in the project
number 15798 and then press the green button.
The system will be activated and you will be
transported back in time.

When you arrive in the past, there will be a pile
of clothes nearby that are suitable for the time
and place, and you must put these on as quickly
as possible.

The people you meet will either mistake you for
someone they know or will not be surprised that
a stranger is with them. On your journeys you
will find that you can help people, this you

should do. Never do anything unkind.

<Return Journey>
When it is time for you to return, you will feel the phone vibrating. You will have to take off the clothes that you've been wearing and leave them in a pile, preferably somewhere they cannot be seen too easily. Take the phone out of the bag and press the red button. If you need to return because of danger before the phone vibrates, key in 15798, remove the clothes as described above and press the red button. This should only be done under real emergency conditions.

<After Your Visit>
We will contact you after your visit to give you an assessment of how well you have done in providing information and living in the time zone which you have visited. We are able to access any part of your computer, so if you would like to write a record about your journey, that would be very helpful but we know you have school work,so if you do not want to do that, that is fine.

We will be sending you a blue screen with an option for travel in the next few days. If you do not take up the option for this or the next two option times, we will assume that you have decided to decline our invitation and we will return your mobile to its original state and retrieve our travel bag.

The screen cleared and then the words 'Goodbye for now' appeared.

CHAPTER 4

Time-Travelling: First Stop
The Year 1615

It was not until two days later that Danny felt his phone vibrating with a quick staccato pulse it had never had before. He was standing in his bedroom having just got back from football and needing a shower. He flicked open his phone and the screen went a vivid blue. This is it, he thought, adrenalin rushing to his head. He went over to his top drawer and took out the small, flat brown bag that had arrived on the shelf beside the elephant moneybox the day before.

He forced himself to walk calmly into the bathroom and lock the door. His hand shaking, he keyed in
15798 and pressed the black button. This time the
screen enlarged only to around the size of an exercise
book.

The message read:

Hello Danny so glad you've decided to go.

(Steady on a moment, I've only pressed the black
button, not the green button, thought Danny. He was
not at all sure he would have the courage to actually
press the green button, but curiosity was raging.)

Then he read:

<Details of Current Travel Option>

<Time Zone>
August 1615.

<Place>
Northern England, inland, country estate.

<Landing>
Two miles from destination.

<Instructions>

Turn towards woods and follow the path; walk through woods towards large house.

<Destination>

Manor house, already over 200 years old.

<Conditions>

Favourable - weather benign – no war, riot or up-rising – no pestilence or illness – no extreme poverty – Disagreements, negligible.

<Equipment>

Mobile phone, travel bag. Mobile phone fitted with beam of light activated when t-o-r-c-h is keyed in (only use sparingly).

If you wish to travel, do as follows:

> take off your clothes, except for underpants
> press the time/space travel bag close to your body so that it is attached: key in 15798
> press the green button.

Have a good trip.

That was all. Danny read the instructions over and over until he knew them off by heart. Each time he read 'Have a good trip' he wanted to laugh. It sounded so everyday, so ordinary as if he were off to Blackpool for the day. He got undressed and pressed the travel bag to his side as he had been instructed. Sure enough it stuck there as if glued on. With a sudden spurt of determination, Danny dialled 15798. Then he pressed the green button. He heard a faint high-pitched whine, far off but coming nearer. Then nothing.

Danny landed with what seemed to him to be a bump, but it wasn't really. One moment he was standing in his underpants in the bathroom, his phone in his hand and the strange bag stuck to his tummy, the next moment he was sitting on a large tussock of grass in a field.

The first thing he noticed was the birds' song which seemed to come from all around and then the sound of crickets chirping and the low hum of bees. The grass was thick and deep and dotted with wild flowers of every kind, homes for a myriad of insects. A bee that had just bumbled out of a nearby flower landed on his nose so that he had to flap at it to get it to buzz off. He felt incredibly happy, as if he had arrived in paradise. The sky was blue with soft white clouds drifting by; 'Simpson clouds' thought Danny.

He looked around for his clothes. Nothing. In front of him was a track leading straight across the field of tufty grass towards a wooded area some way off. He remembered the instructions. 'Turn towards the wood and follow the path.' He just hadn't realised that he would have to do that before he found his clothes.

He got up and started walking down the path in the direction of the woods. He was just beginning to wonder if he was doing the right thing when the path dipped down into a hollow. Beside a stream that ran along the length of this lower ground, on a large flat boulder there was a bundle of what looked like garments. He ran up to the pile. Yes it was clothes. The first things he picked up were two grey woollen stockings.

"Oh Pleas..ease – surely I don't have to put these on?" Danny said the words out loud to the empty air so great was his disgust, and then realising that no one was going to answer, he struggled into each stocking. He stood holding the tops up wondering what next when he spotted two long lengths of string. He managed to secure the stockings by tying the string round the tops of his legs.

Next, he put on a pair of very baggy pants that came to his knees and billowed out like pantaloons. He started giggling to himself at the thought of what he must look like. Then he put on a grey item that looked as if it had once been white. It had something of a frilly collar so he supposed it was a shirt, but there was no opening down the front. He pulled it on over his head. The last item of clothing was a cross between a tunic and a jacket. It was made out of a thick material that was possibly of a good quality although it had obviously seen better days. It was a dark blue and had no collar so he pulled the collar from the shirt out over the top.

The clothes were all very itchy and smelt of something unpleasant. He had a nasty suspicion that this was because they needed a good wash, which made him very glad that he had still got on his own underpants.

All that was left were two strangely shaped shoes each made of what looked like two pieces of leather roughly sewn together. The leather on the sole was quite hard, whereas on the upper part, it was as soft as material. There were two long leather thongs coming from the back of the shoe. He bent down and tied these round his ankle. The shoes felt really floppy as if they would come off after a few steps, so he tried again and lashed the thongs under his foot. They were much tighter after that and actually felt quite comfortable.

Then, as he stood up, a dreadful, fearful realisation flashed into his mind like a knife cutting through soft tissue. He had left his mobile behind where he had landed in the field. He had just not bothered to pick it up!

With a terror he had never known in his life before, he ran back up to the higher ground. He stopped when he reached the flat field and looked ahead. How would he find the spot where he had landed?

Even though he desperately wanted to run ahead, he made himself walk slowly back along the path, his eyes glued to the ground. Dreadful thoughts filled his mind; he had failed on his first attempt, he would be stranded in 1615, and he would never see his mum and dad again. His mouth was dry with fear and his stomach churned in the most horrible way. Then a short distance in front of him he saw a dog, a small brown and white spaniel, not much more than a puppy. It was snuffling and sniffing at something on the ground. When he got closer he could see what it was – it was his phone! With a tremendous cry of relief, he bent down to pick it up and the little dog started licking him and jumping up with great excitement as if he were a long lost friend.

"Steady on little chap, I'm very grateful to you for finding my phone but I've got one or two things to do now. I should have done them when I first got here but everything went out of my head." Danny sat down and fished around under his new smelly clothes until he found the time travel bag. How on earth had he managed to forget about it and all the instructions? It was as if his mind had gone blank the minute he had landed in the field. He got the thin silver disc out of the bag and pressed it to his forehead. The back fell away leaving a thin film on his brow. For a moment he felt a cold sensation and then nothing. He ran his hand across his forehead, it felt perfectly smooth as if a piece of sticking plaster had vanished into his skin. He carefully put the mobile and the outer case of the disc into the bag and pressed the flap shut. The bag with the mobile in it hugged the side of his body as though it was stuck there with super glue; he couldn't feel it at all, even with the weight of the phone in it. He got up and walked down the path towards the wood, the little dog following.

He quickly arrived at the spot by the stream

where his clothes had been. Now he needed to get across to the other side. Danny looked down at the spaniel.

"I'm not sure you should follow me, old chap. If you follow me, you could be walking away from your home." The dog sat looking up at him, wagging his tail as best he could against the ground.

"Go home, go home." Danny pointed in the direction from which they had come. He gave the dog a shove. No response at all, except for a sad and sorrowful gaze from its large brown eyes. It was obvious the dog was going nowhere without him.

"Oh well, you'd best come along, I suppose." Danny petted him behind his ears and was rewarded by another bout of happy yapping and licking.

The stream, which was shallow, was quite wide and fast-flowing in places but it was not going to give him a problem. Large stones had been placed strategically all the way across. Danny managed to step from stone to stone to the other side without getting his strange leather slippers wet. The dog didn't follow, but whined pitifully from the bank. In the end Danny went back, picked him up and carried him across. On the other side once again, he put the dog down and made his way up a steep bank, the dog at his heels.

When he got to the top, he could see that he was only a few yards from the edge of the woodland. He was soon walking among tall trees that shut out much of the light. There were huge oaks and smaller conifers, and in some places saplings that grew so close together they made an impenetrable thicket. It was obvious that someone had felled trees to allow travellers to pass along this woodland track. Even though Danny had never been in such a dense wood before on his own, he did not feel afraid. Quite the contrary, he felt light-hearted as if he had come back to somewhere he knew really well.

At one point, he came to a clearing where there was a hut, or maybe it was a very small house. Beside it there were huge piles of thick logs and smaller piles of sticks. Grandmother's cottage he joked to himself. Perhaps I will meet Red Riding Hood soon. After the woodcutter's cottage, if that's what it was, the path widened out quite a bit. In places it was rather boggy. He could see the marks of cart wheels where they had gone down in the mud. Danny walked quickly, remembering the instructions that had said he would have to go two miles to reach the Destination.

The little dog was tiring and he had started limping. Without thinking, Danny bent down to pick him up and the little creature snuggled into his arm as if that was what he had been after all the time.

After about twenty minutes, the trees thinned and he emerged from the gloom of the wood into the sunlight. A few yards in front of him the path crossed a much wider track, almost a road, Danny thought. The idea was confirmed by the sight of a man on a big sturdy horse, trotting away from him to his right.

He wondered for a moment if he should go left or right along this wider road and then decided no, the instructions had said 'straight ahead.' In front of him was a beautiful view, a wide meadowland dotted with ponies and small brown cattle. To his right meandered a small river and then directly in front of him, still quite a way off, a large house, standing high on a steep slope. A mansion house had been given as his 'Destination.' That must be it, Danny thought and he carried on straight ahead.

As he drew near, he began for the first time to feel apprehensive. The house looked so huge, so imposing; tall brick chimneys soared above gable-ended roofs, thick beams criss-crossed the plastered walls and the glass in its many tall windows reflected back the sunlight. What was he supposed to do once he had reached his destination? For the first time he realised that SHARP had said nothing about that. The path now bore round to the left taking him to one side of the house.

Suddenly from close behind, Danny heard a cry:

"Hey Edmond is that you?" He turned to see a lad slightly taller than himself coming towards him down an adjoining path. Remembering what SHARP had said about meeting people in the changed time zone, Danny realised that this boy was mistaking him for someone else.

"Err yes, that's me." he replied rather sheepishly, feeling a fraud and carrying on walking; he wasn't sure what else to do. The lad drew level with him and walked along beside him in a friendly way.

"Thank heavens you have the little dog. Why, your life wouldn't be worth living if you had not found Mistress Dorothy's Beauty. Not a name for a dog if you ask me, but then no one is ever likely to are they?"

Not knowing quite what to say to this, Danny looked down at the little dog in his arms and gave her a tickle under the chin, getting lots of licks for his trouble. Despite himself, he giggled, leaning his face away as much as he could.

"They tell me in the kitchen that Mistress Dorothy has forsaken her needlework all day long, pining for her Beauty." The lad chatted on happily, not noticing that Danny was not saying anything.

They rounded a corner at the side of the house and arrived in a large courtyard. It looked a busy place. There were piles of wood, neat rows of barrels, huge rakes, shovels, buckets and various other tools that Danny couldn't identify. There was a large door leading into the house. Danny stopped, not knowing quite what to do and turned towards his new companion.

"Here. Do you want to take…er…Beauty for me?" (He was going to say 'the dog' but stopped himself and managed to use the dog's proper name.)

"Don't be silly. You must take Beauty up to her. She sent you out to look for her and she will want you, Edmond to bring what was lost to her. You are such a strange one, you know. Everyone likes you and yet you never want to take the glory for anything. I can't make you out at all at times."

During this little speech Danny's eyes had wandered to the upper elevation of the building. Perhaps this was a mistake because suddenly he saw it; the small curved window with the carving underneath – a fat angel standing on the head of a man with branches of a tree coming out of his mouth. He stared transfixed. He had been here, at this spot, this very spot, talking to his dad only a few days ago! He felt himself go dizzy.

"Edmond what are you staring at so?" The boy shook him. "Stop staring at the Green Man. It'll do you no good. Ever since you came to the Davenports as their squire, you've worried about that carving up there."

"I just wonder what it means." Danny tried his best to pull himself together; he could see the lad was getting upset.

"Nothing. That's what it means. God knows what them strange lot, 200 years ago thought when they put that there. I wish the Master would take it down. He and Mistress Dorothy have done so much to the house but not touched that. They say it would show disrespect for the Bromales. I, Dan Pacey, am supposed to have descent from them on my mother's side. But do you know what Edmond?" The boy gave him a little shake again and stopped talking, waiting for a response. Danny, amused now that his new acquaintance had the same name as him, smiled at him broadly:

"No Dan Pacey, I don't know what."

"I'm so glad I live now. Why, in them days, they

had all sorts of stupid ideas and they didn't even have glass in the windows of a big house like this. They were backward and useless, that's what I say."

Danny laughed out loud now. partly because he still found it funny that this lad was called Dan and partly at the thought that his new friend considered glass in windows such an innovation.

"Mmm, things have really moved on," he said with a sarcasm that only he understood. "But you mustn't dis the past you know." Danny looked into the honest, kind face of his new friend and was suddenly struck by the thought that he reminded him of Mark.

"Dis?" asked Dan Pacey puzzled.

"Oh that's a word I've made up meaning show disrespect."

"Making up your own words now! If you're not careful you'll end up a poet, Master Edmond. But you had better go on in and get that dog up to Mistress Dorothy. I've to be off home now." The boy turned away and strode purposefully across the yard towards a small pony tied up at a post. With one bound he landed on the pony's bare back. He leant forward, un-tying the tether from the post and pulled the pony round to trot out of the yard.

"Wait, Dan." Danny shouted, not wanting to see

him go.

"What is it Edmond?" the lad pulled his pony up to listen.

"Thank you, thank you for being a help."

"Oh I'll always be here to help you Edmond." The lad waved merrily and shouted a 'goodbye' as he clattered out of the yard.

After the sound of the pony's hooves had faded, Danny stared up at the strange carving.

"That's odd," he said as if he was talking to the angel and tree man, "even in 1615 people thought you were out-of-date, and yet there you are still staring out at the twenty-first century people." Danny's ideas about history were changing by the minute.

Not knowing what to do next, he pushed open the large door in front of him and stepped cautiously round into the interior of Bramall Hall. A tall ornately-carved screen blocked the way immediately in front of him, but a few steps to one side and he found himself in a huge hall. In a massive stone fireplace, logs the thickness of whole trees smouldered gently, glowing with red embers at their base and sending small spirals of smoke up the great chimney. In the middle of the room, there was a huge table with a tall, imposing chair at one end and benches down the sides. There were some smaller tables, also with benches, and on one there were piles of plates and drinking tankards. There was no one around. He was about to put the little dog down and go, when a girl about Jenny's size, hurtled through a door and raced towards him across the stone floor. She was wearing a dress that went from her chin right down to her ankles and seemed to be made of a very stiff material, but that didn't slow her down.

"You've found Beauty, Oh Edmond, you've found Beauty." She flung her arms round him. "Come and take her up to grandma, she has been pining for her so."

Fortunately for Danny, the girl had no intention of letting him go on his own. She held his hand and half skipping, half running led him across the hall, through a dark passageway and up a wide staircase, chattering all the while about how she had searched all day for the missing Beauty without any success. On the first floor the girl led him through a landing and a small room and then stopped at a door and held her finger to her lips, not that Danny had been responsible for any of the noise; it had all been of her making. She gently pushed open the door and stood back to let Danny go in.

Sitting opposite him on the other side of the large room was a very upright, elderly lady. Her clothes were ornate, tucked and embellished with bright stitching. At her neck she wore a large, stiff lace ruff. Her face, though old and wrinkled, was calm and imposing. No one would disobey her. Danny had never seen anyone like her in his life. His steps faltered. She had a needle in her hand, and in front of her an oval shape on a stand held a piece of embroidery. She bent forward and tucked her needle safely away before turning to face him.

"Come, come Edmond. Come forward, whatever is the matter with you?"

"I've found Beauty." He said, unsure of what else he could possibly say.

"I can see that, but why don't you put her down?" Her voice was harsh and abrupt.

"She was limping. I think she's hurt her paw, perhaps that's why she couldn't get home."

"Oh the poor dear thing!" The change in the lady was immediate. She swept over to them and pressed Danny and the little dog to her bosom, a total shock to Danny's system. Fortunately, the unbearably close contact didn't last long. She let them go, then scooped Beauty up out of his arms. She took the little dog back to her seat and Danny saw that Beauty was giving her the full licking treatment. Then he had an idea.

"I think she probably needs a drink."

"Of course, what a sensible boy you are. Off you go to the kitchen and get one of them to bring up a bowl of water and a dish of meat."

Danny turned to go, not sure whether he should bow or whatever when he left her presence. He needn't have worried because the lady was so engrossed in her precious dog that she didn't look up. But before he left the room he heard her call:

"Edmond."

He stopped, "Yes…(help what title should he use?) Mistress Dorothy." It must have been correct.

"Edmond," she repeated the name more softly. "I am most pleased with you." She smiled at him. "Now be quick to the kitchens."

He flushed with pride at this praise, just as if he was the real Edmond!

When he got outside the door, the girl was nowhere to be seen. How would he find the kitchens now? Well, they must be downstairs he supposed. He descended the stairs slowly, trying to gather his thoughts as to the usual arrangements for such things – probably next to the dining hall. Was that the dining hall he had first come through? At the bottom of the stairs, he nearly bumped into a scruffy girl with rough, reddened hands carrying a bowl of water and a dish of meat.

"Oh Master Edmond, Missy Annie said that Mistress Dorothy wanted water and meat for Beauty." Danny realised that Missy Annie must have been listening at the door and run ahead of him to the kitchens. Well, that was lucky.

The girl looked as if she were about to pass the things she was carrying to him. Danny held up his hand to stop her.

"You take it up to her," he said. He looked at her. She was a sorry, thin thing with straggly hair and a pinched face. He suddenly knew that she was one of the people who did not have much fun living in this big, beautiful house.

"You know there is way too much meat there for a little dog to eat. I should take a bit off, if I was you." He winked at her.

"Oh Master Edmond," she exclaimed. She passed him and went on up the stairs quickly. Looking up, he could tell that she had stopped, no doubt to put a few pieces of the meat into her own mouth and gobble them down quickly before she got to the Mistress's room. He went along the dark passageway that led back to the hall. It was darker now as evening was beginning to set in. Suddenly there was a rustling sound and Annie jumped out of a shadowy doorway.

"Annie you gave me a shock," he said, amazed at how easily he used the names of these people he had never met before.

"And so I should Edmond, after all you have been so very unkind to me."

"Why? What have I done?"

"You very well know – not taking me with you on your search for Beauty."

"Well, you would've slowed me down. It took me a long time to find Beauty; she had strayed so far away. You would have soon got tired."

"I would not. Just remember, I will get you back for not taking me." She looked up at him laughing as if to reassure him that she was not serious in her intentions. "But now I have something to show you."

"What is that?"

"Something, you've been so curious about. Something you've been nagging me about." She paused to give dramatic effect to her next statement.

"I've found out how to get into the priest's room. What do you think about that?" She said this with great triumph in her voice.

"Really?"

"Yes, really. Come back upstairs with me and I'll show you."

"Oh no. Not today. I've had a hard day. What about tomorrow?"

"I know you must be hungry Edmond, after being out all day, but it will only take a minute. You are always so curious. You know I won't show you another time. Only today."

"Go on then. But I mustn't be long."

She clapped her hands delightedly and skipped up the stairs in front of him. Danny followed to the landing where they were before, but this time they turned to the right and went through a different door. He found himself in a room with a four-poster bed.

"Surely we are not supposed to be in here?"

"No one will come in here for ages. Come over here. Look Edmond, by the fireplace. The third panel up is a slightly different wood, and if you touch it you can feel it is a loose panel." She paused while Danny looked as interested as possible. "If you press hard on it, it comes away." She did this and the small panel came loose. "And there is the latch." She pointed to something that looked like a notch in the wood.

With a creaking sound, that made Danny shiver, a small door swung open to reveal a space behind. "Look in there – there's a chair and a bed. Don't you think I have been clever to find it?"

"Yes, very clever." Half out of curiosity and half to please her, Danny went over and peered into the completely dark space. He could just make out a narrow bed and a wooden chair. Next thing, Annie had given him a shove and, in his surprise, he tumbled forward into the pitch black room. She laughed as she banged the door shut. He was in complete darkness.

'Wow,' he thought, 'she was well annoyed with Edmond for leaving her behind.' He waited for a while expecting that she would soon let him out. But clearly that was not in her plan. For a moment he felt a surge of panic, and thought of dialling the emergency number. Then he began to get control of his fear and decided against it. He would like to get the better of Miss Annie himself, without the help from greater powers.

Surely there must be a latch this side of the door? He patted up and down the wall but couldn't feel a thing. The intense blackness was making him feel a bit strange. Then he remembered the torch function on his phone. He fished around under his clothes and got the mobile out of its bag and switched it on. Amazingly, the familiar screen lit up. He began to feel like James Bond who always had some gadget with him to get him out of tight spots. According to instructions he keyed in t-o-r-c-h.

A small but bright beam came from the end. Brilliant. He shone it up and down the piece of wall where he thought the door should be and what do you know? He didn't have to look for a hidden notch or anything. Because there was no need for secrecy on this side, there was a perfectly visible latch, rather a small latch and high up, almost out of his reach, but a latch just the same. So much for Annie's little plan to lock him away forever! He stretched up, pressed the latch, pushed hard and the door swung out, making its now familiar creaking sound. Relieved, he stepped out. Despite his desire to get away quickly, he couldn't help casting a look around at the room with its strange four-poster bed hung with heavy curtains. The room was quite bare, with just a huge chest and a chair with a small stool in front of it. He walked quietly out of the door, along the passage and broke into a run down the stairs. He could feel his phone vibrating.

Time for him to go. But where was she? He couldn't go without letting the little trickster know he had foiled her plans. When he got to the great hall, he paused in the doorway. She was sitting on a small stool by the fire with her back to him. He tiptoed across the hall and when he got nearly to the wooden screen by the outside door, he called out:

"Hey Annie, I won't forget you in a hurry."

She turned round with a jump. "Edmond. My goodness! How on earth did you get out so quickly? You know, I was only saying every rhyme I knew and then I would have come and let you out."

"Oh I couldn't wait that long. You know so many rhymes." He wanted to say goodbye, wanted to say he thought she was lots of fun, and that if she waited a few hundred years she wouldn't have to put up with being treated differently to boys. But he knew he couldn't do that, so he just pushed open the door and went outside. Even though the sun was beginning to set, it was much lighter outside than in the gloom of the large house.

He went round the side of the building the way he had walked earlier with Dan, and came upon a thick clump of bushes where he would be hidden from view. He took off his clothes and left them in a pile just as he had found them, the grey woollen stockings on the top. He shivered with the cold of the evening air, but paused for a minute to take one last look at the massive walls of Bramall Hall in the gathering darkness of 1615. Then he dialled 15798 and pressed the red button. It never even occurred to him to worry about the return journey.

He arrived back in the bathroom and Jenny was knocking on the door.

"Hurry up Danny, it's time for tea." called his sister.

CHAPTER 5

Time Slip

Hurry up for tea. TEA? He had just been talking to people who lived 393 years ago; he had been wearing smelly clothes that someone else had been wearing 393 years ago; his face had been licked all over by a little dog that belonged to the 393 years ago people. How could he just go downstairs and have tea? But that is what he did, and nobody in his family noticed (well not then) that he was any different from his usual self. But Danny was different.

In the days that followed his amazing journey back in time, Danny's mind seemed to be elsewhere, his thoughts swimming about in a liquid form inside his head unable to fix on any one point or form into a solid idea. When he did come to for a bit, he felt as if he was encapsulated in an invisible bubble, separated from people by an unseen barrier, alone in his experience of being the only person on earth to travel through time and space. He kept wondering whether his phone was going to vibrate and tell him that a second journey was planned. He must have looked down at its screen a hundred times in one day. Caught between feeling very strangely detached from the world around him and a spiralling excitement about where, and to what time zone, he might travel to next, his powers of concentration were non-existent. After a while, people started to notice.

At school, his teachers were puzzled. Danny Higgins, who was usually so good at concentrating on his work, appeared to be in a daydream. When they asked him a question, he would jump, as if he had not been listening. Then, the slightly annoyed teacher would have to repeat the question and Danny would come up with a lacklustre answer as if he didn't care whether he was right or wrong.

But there was a worse problem: his football skills had sunk to zero.

"What's up with you, mate?" Mark had shouted at him after Danny had played badly during the match against St. Benedict's. Haybury Comprehensive, Mark and Danny's school, had only just managed to equalize at the last minute in this match. They always beat St. Benedict's.

"That goal was wide open and you missed! Even a girl could've got that one in." Mark glowered.

"You ran like a...like a...(not very good with

words, Mark couldn't think of a sufficiently stinging insult) "like a duck" was what he finally came out with. In the normal way Danny would have laughed at this and retaliated instantly, but this time he didn't even raise an eyebrow. He just stared at Mark vacantly.

"It's like you're not here, mate." Mark shook his head as if in despair at the change in his friend.

Among Danny's teachers, most thought: 'Oh dear, Danny Higgins is going through a rough patch, maybe he has fallen for a girl or something – he'll no doubt pick up in a few weeks.' But Mrs Cartwright who taught maths was very concerned. She knew Danny's mum from a reading group that they both belonged to. She picked up the phone and dialled the number of the Higgins' home.

"Is that Rachel Higgins? It's Susan Cartwright here…No I haven't called about the next meeting of the reading group. I'm sorry to bother you, but I am very worried about Danny's work. It's really gone downhill in the last few weeks. I was wondering, do you know of anything that might be bothering him?"

Danny's mum had just got back from the Thursday evening swim with Jenny. Danny hadn't wanted to come, and this in itself had been worrying. That evening Danny's mum and dad had a chat with him.

Because they never got cross or angry with their children, they started off by telling him how pleased they had always been with him, how they knew he always worked hard and how they knew he would never get into any sort of trouble, but that IF he did, they knew he would tell them. Then they started to look concerned and his Dad almost appeared cross. He looked, Danny thought absentmindedly, as if he were holding in a serious explosion and didn't dare open his mouth.

"We are really worried about your work at school, Danny. Is there something you want to tell us?" His mother leant across and took hold of his hand. "Are you being bullied or…or?" Danny knew that she wanted to say something more but couldn't bring herself to even think that he was involved in stuff like nicking things or drugs with the scally boys at his school – as if.

Danny just sat still and stared ahead blankly. He didn't even shift about uncomfortably, which he would have done in the normal way when having such a conversation with his parents. He managed to say that there was nothing worrying him and that he would try harder with his school work.

"But Danny, I don't think it is about you working harder," said his worried Mum "You just don't seem

to be here."

That night before he went to sleep, Jenny came into his room and sat cross-legged at the bottom of his bed. She gave him a long lecture, listing all the things he had failed to do over the last few weeks. She had noticed something his Mum and Dad, with their own pre-occupations, had failed to notice:

"And Danny! Just look at your room. It's untidy. In all the years I've been alive, you have never had an untidy room." Her face was creased with a worried frown. "It's like you're not my brother any more. You are the best brother in the world Danny, and you would tell me wouldn't you if anything is wrong? Even if you don't tell the grown ups, you would tell me wouldn't you?"

Of course that got to him. His teachers' annoyed comments had floated over his head, his parents' well-meaning words had hardly been heard, even Mark's anger hadn't penetrated his defences, but Jenny made him sit up startled.

"It's like you've been taken by aliens." Trust Jenny to get it nearly right. Danny gave himself a shake and suddenly felt as if he had emerged back into the twenty-first century. The awful feeling of being suspended in a vacuum seemed to vanish. His swimmy thoughts were coming together into some kind of sense. His sister who had seemed as if she was a two-dimensional figure at the start of the conversation suddenly seemed very real.

"Look Jenny. I have had something on my mind – but you really mustn't worry. Promise me you won't worry."

"I won't worry if you tell me what it is. Are you getting in with the wrong people?"

"It's nothing like that, believe me. Just trust me Jenny. Everything is fine. I can't tell you about it, not yet. I will do one day, I promise."

Jenny gave him a big hug and Danny hugged her back. He really wished he could tell her about his adventures; how amazed she would be, and she of all people would believe him. But he knew that he must not do that. Jenny got off his bed and padded out of his room, poking her head round his door just before she closed it:

"Now, no turning back into that horrid flat person by the morning, will you Danny?"

"I won't Jenny. You have rescued me." He grinned. Strange but she had. He felt fine, just like his old self. All he was worrying about now was that a blue screen had not come up on his phone to alert him

to a new adventure back in time. Had he been so rubbish on his last trip that SHARP had decided not to use
him again? What about their promise to get in touch
with him to tell him how well he had done on that
trip? It was over a month now since his journey to 1615
and he had not had any communication from them at
all.

The next day, just after he had got back from
school and started on his home work, Danny felt his
phone vibrating. There was the familiar brilliant blue
screen hovering just a few feet away from the phone
and a message from Kaz.

Hi Danny, glad to see you are feeling better. If
you go to your computer I can send you messages just the same as on your phone but you
can type in your messages for me.

Danny went over and switched his computer on.
The same message that had been on his phone filled
the screen and at the bottom there was a button on
which the words: 'post your reply' appeared.

He sat down and typed a little angrily: I've been
feeling really awful after I got back.

I know. I'm really sorry but I didn't realize you were going to get time slip so badly.

Time slip? typed in Danny.

Yeah it's like people travelling across the world in aeroplanes in your period would say they had jet lag. Time slip is really common but usually it only lasts for a few hours, sometimes only minutes, like it did with you, when you first landed. Professor Aurelia Dobbs is trying to work out why it was so bad for you on the return. She thinks it's because you did so well and you really made the most of your journey.

I did well? queried Danny, excited now.

Oh yes exceptionally well, everyone was crowding round the pictures that came back – they were so clear and we heard everything. Some people's sound and pictures are really indistinct: it all depends on how well you fit in to the time and place, even to how the people you meet respond to you. If they don't believe in you, it messes with the transmission. You were great

Danny, just as if you had had training. I mean there are chaps who've had six months training for their trips back in time who don't do as well as you on their first time.

So I'll be able to go again?

Oh definitely.

For a moment Danny sat looking at the word 'definitely' and felt his excitement rising. He had really convinced himself he would not be going on any more SHARP journeys.

That's fantastic, he typed pausing before tapping the 'post your reply' button. Then he typed: I've been wondering: does the Destination have to be a place you've visited in your own time zone?

You catch on fast Danny, as I have said before. That is exactly it and the closer in time the two trips are, the better, although that doesn't always matter too much. Up to a three or four year gap is the best in general.

Oh, I see. You know that I forgot to follow the instructions when I first landed. It was as if I was in a daydream.

Yes, that was caused by time slip as well. I should be apologising to you Danny. I forgot to warn you. But you know now.

Yes and I'll be prepared for it next time. Now I know about it.

Sure Danny. I'm sorry I forgot to tell you. The thing is it's something SHARP people are constantly researching and, as I said, some people get it much worse than others. I have lost marks because I forgot to tell you.

Oh Kaz, I'm really sorry about that.

Don't be. I've gained loads of marks otherwise because you did so well. I could even end up with honours.

Danny smiled to himself. It was really strange thinking about Kaz worrying about his exam results while he went spinning through time and space.

I bet there are lots of things you have to think about when I get to go on a trip.

You want to believe it. There's a whole range of instrument panels in front of me, and all sorts. Anyway, the current research from SHARP on time slip is that if you feel any symptoms, either on landing in a new time zone or returning to your own, focus hard on the immediate environment, on what you can see, hear and even smell and you should become more stabilised. I've got to post out now Danny. Huge congratulations. You did very, very well. I have just got to formally ask you: do you want a second trip? You must just answer Yes or No.

Yes.

After that, the screen went blank and Danny sat looking at it for a while. Then he got up and started jumping up and down and throwing things in the air. Then he let out a wild whoop of joy. Jenny pushed his door open.

"Have you gone loopy?" She stared wide-eyed at her bouncing brother who had now landed on his bed and was trying to do trampoline manoeuvres, still letting out triumphant shouts.

Seeing that Jenny was still looking worried, Danny calmed down and sat down on the edge of the bed.

"It's okay Jen. It's just that I'm back to my old self and I am really happy about that." As if to prove to her that this was the case he got up and started tidying his room, putting clothes away in the dirty bin and books back on shelves. This had an immediate effect. Jenny gave a huge sigh of relief. Then a big grin came over her face and she said:

"That's all right, then. I'm so glad, I can go and untidy my room."

"What?"

"Well I thought that seeing's you had gone all strange and started being untidy, if I changed and went from untidy to tidy it might sort of put things right. Maybe it did work. What do you think? You're back to normal now."

"Jenny, seven-year-old girl logic is really crap. It's far stranger than I ever was. But, well I suppose you never know. Maybe it did work."

Most seven-year-old girls would have started a quarrel with their ungrateful brother at this point but

Jenny just said: "Danny, crap isn't a nice word to use," and left.

Danny carried on tidying up his room. Amazing, he thought, how much junk accumulates in a couple of weeks if you're an untidy sod. Then a very good idea came to him. He sat down on his computer and found a blog site that kids could use. He started writing about his journey back in time to 1615 to the Hall at Bramhall village, Cheshire.

CHAPTER 6

Doublet And Hose

That evening when the family were having dinner, Mr and Mrs Higgins kept sharing meaningful looks and little smiles and nods. It all meant that they had noticed that Danny seemed to be back to his old self.

Then, when Jenny had just eaten the last forkful of Mrs. Higgins's tasty, but often served, dish of vegetable lasagne, she said in a loud voice:

"Danny's back to his old self now. His room's tidy again."

Everyone laughed.

"Jenny, we were trying not to make it too obvious that we had noticed," said Mum.

"Oh," said Jenny, puzzled by this seemingly unnecessary pretence by the grown-ups. Danny gave her a grin.

"It was Jenny who rescued me," he told the parents.

"How come?" asked Dad whose turn it was now to be puzzled.

"Well, you are never going to believe this, but the reason I've been a bit odd just lately is because I've taken up a new hobby, a very absorbing new hobby." He looked round at the three of them, all waiting to hear his next words.

"I'm writing a book," he paused for effect, no need to worry he had everyone's undivided attention, "and I never realised how it takes up so much of one's mind. I mean it totally takes over your thinking processes." He was in full flight now with this splendid fabrication. His parents' expressions were worthy of posting on YouTube; his Mum looking as if she had won a lottery prize and his Dad as if he couldn't believe his ears. "I'd got stuck, absolutely stuck at one point, and then Jenny came to talk to me and said: 'it's like you've been taken by aliens' and that was the clue I had been looking for."

"Clue you'd been looking for?" His mum and dad repeated in unison. "Are you writing a science fiction story?" Their disappointment, after near delight, was tangible. Danny knew they hated science fiction, so what he said next was really crucial.

"Well no, it's not science fiction at all, really. I'm writing stories set in the past, the Tudor, Elizabethan or Stuart Period, those sort of times, but I was strug-

gling to think of a way to make it interesting for kids who ..who ," how could he put this and still keep them happy? "...have no grasp of history." He couldn't tell if this last bit had gone down well or not as both his parents' eyebrows had shot up in the most comical fashion and their mouths had fallen slightly open when Danny had said the words 'Tudor, Elizabethan or Stuart' and by the end of his sentence, their eyebrows were still up and their mouths still open. Danny looked at Jenny and could see that she was having terrible trouble not to laugh.

"Tudor, Elizabethan, Stuart!" they exclaimed in unison again, after managing to get their eyebrows down and mouths closed.

"Yes, I thought those would be very interesting times." Danny went on wickedly, saying the very thing that was likely to send the eyebrows up again, but this time both parents managed to keep their facial features in check. Danny continued: "the thing was, I couldn't work out a good way to make that period accessible to the modern child, so I thought of sending a twenty-first century boy back to the sixteenth or seventeenth century to have an adventure and this is where the aliens had to come in. They have the scientific knowledge to make that happen."

"Wow," said Jenny. "It sounds a really exciting story. Can I read it?"

"Well, not yet Jenny. You know authors who show people their work before it is finished, never do get it finished."

Several years earlier, Mrs. Higgins had had a book published about a very obscure happening in the thirteenth century. It had been much praised in academic circles, but it had sold no more than fifty copies or so, mainly to friends and relations. Nevertheless, as a published author, it ensured that she was an expert on the writing processes and she quickly agreed with Danny on this point.

"I know just what you are feeling, Danny," she said. "When you are going through the creative process of writing a book, it's as if you have been extracted from this world. And I totally agree with you about not wanting anyone looking at it until it is finished. I for one, wouldn't dream of asking you to show me your manuscript." Danny smiled his thanks at his mum, having known all along what her reaction would be.

Mr. Higgins, while making a note that at some later time he must discuss with Danny his firmly held belief that time travel was a physical impossibility, congratulated Danny on this newly-acquired, but quite unexpected, interest in history. Then he said:

"Now Jenny, I think you had better be getting off upstairs to bed, and Danny, haven't you some homework to do?"

The parents couldn't wait to get their two children out of the room so that they could discuss this new development, Danny's sudden, inexplicable interest in their favourite subject – history. They would be mulling over it for the rest of the evening.

"Well, I have finished my homework, but I do want to get on with my writing now."

"Don't let it interfere with your school work, will you son?"

"No worries Dad. Oh by the way Mum, I was wondering, what is the correct term for that strange sort of jacket thing that went over those stockings and puffy pants that men and boys wore in Tudor times? I'm sure there's a name for those clothes."

"The term is a doublet and hose, Danny."

"Thanks mum. Can I come to you for any other bits of information?"

"Of course, you can."

Just as Danny had thought, Mr.and Mrs. Higgins sat for ages mulling over Danny's new found interest in history.

"After him being so bored, so often, in almost every museum we've ever visited, I just can't believe that this evening he asked me the term for a doublet and hose," said Mrs. Higgins happily.

Two days later when Danny got in from school, and Mum and Jenny were out shopping, SHARP contacted him.

Hello Danny! Here are the instructions for your second trip back in time. I do hope you can take this option and all goes as well as last time.

Danny thought about it for a moment. He would be in the house on his own for at least another hour. Mum had taken Jenny to buy a new pair of shoes; it was always a lengthy business. Shivers of excitement tinged with fear began to race up and down his body. His hand started to shake so much he had trouble holding the phone. Would this trip be as trouble free as last time? Could he do it? Would he remember everything?

He sat down and read:

<Details of Current Travel Option>

<Time Zone>
June 1588.

<Place>
Northern England, inland, country farming estate.

<Landing>
Outbuildings possible barn or stable belonging to
Destination.

<Instructions>
After getting dressed, wait until people come to
fetch you.

<Destination>
Manor house, possibly 100 years old.

<Identity>
Known to everyone in the vicinity, the son of the
landowner.

<Conditions>

Favourable – weather benign – no war, riot or up-
rising – no pestilence or illness – no extreme
poverty – Some local disagreement.

<Equipment>
Mobile phone, travel bag. Mobile phone fitted
with beam of light activated when t-o-r-c-h is
keyed in (only use sparingly).
If you wish to travel, do as follows:
> take off your clothes, except for underpants
> press the time/space travel bag close to
  your body so that it is attached: key in
  15798
> press the green button.
Have a good trip.

As he had done last time, Danny read and re-
read the instructions. He noticed that the date was 30
years earlier than before and that there was an entry
giving an identity, though not a name. He got undressed, pressed the bag to his tummy, dialled the
number and then quickly, so as not to change his mind,
pressed the green button. As before, he heard the faint
high-pitched sound, and then nothing.

CHAPTER 7

Time-Travelling: Second Stop
The Year 1588

"Bloomin' heck! SHARP was cutting that fine," Danny exclaimed out loud as he landed, into the world of fifteen hundred and eighty-eight, within a finger-width of the thick wooden walls of what seemed to be a barn. How awful it would be to land on top of a building! Still, it hadn't happened, so no point worrying. He was standing safely in what he supposed was a farmyard. The large brown eyes of cattle with massive, long, sharply pointed horns and shaggy fringes were sleepily observing him from a stall across the untidy yard. A very strong smell of farm manure assaulted his nostrils.

"Whew…I think I'll get out of here as quickly as possible," he said, to the uninterested animals. Danny had obviously forgotten the final instruction to remain where he was until someone came to find him.

SHARP had definitely done better than last time in locating his clothes. There was a pile of garments only a few feet away from him. They were neatly folded and placed on top of a stone block. Danny wondered if it was a mounting block – a lot of riding stables have similar ones to this day. He looked behind him and saw that in a nearby stable a grey horse was eyeing him intently.

"Hello boy, I'll come and pat you in a minute but I think I'd better get dressed first."

He reminded himself that before he did anything, he had to take the small disc out of his time/space travel bag and attach it to his forehead. Like last time, the film on the metal disc seemed to melt into his forehead and he was left with the metal piece to pop into the bag. He was just congratulating himself on how clear-headed he felt, when a dreadful whoozey feeling came over him. Time slip, he thought. This is not good; supposing someone comes into the yard? Remembering Kaz's instructions to make a conscious effort to notice things, he stared hard at his surroundings. They had become indistinct, even the thick solid walls of the barn seemed indistinct and somehow distorted, as if through atmospheric interference. Danny struggled hard to focus.

There were three cattle pens, then a long, low bank of manure, steaming slightly, a stone wall with a thick bed of nettles growing in front, and then a rickety, half-open gate. Big bluebottle flies buzzed around the cattle as they swished their tales and rhythmically chewed the cud. A small bird flew down and perched on one end of the gate. Danny watched the bird, which turned its head this way and that, as if wondering what it should do next. Slowly, Danny's mind began to clear and the edges of objects began to sharpen. He looked down at his right hand. He was still holding his phone. Breathing in deeply, despite the strong smell, he shook off the last of the dizziness and put the mobile into the bag that lay flush against the skin of his stomach and fastened the bag shut.

The clothes were very similar to the ones he had worn last time, except that the pantaloons were bigger and puffed out more. I must be getting used to togging myself out like a complete nutter, he thought as he did up the various ribbons, garters and laces that kept the clothes in place. He was wondering whether people had any buttons in 1588, when he spotted shiny metal ones down the front of the last item, a jacket that had no sleeves. Mmm, I think this is my doublet – very smart. Mum would be proud of me in my 'doublet and hose'. The other thing that was different was a little pouch that hung from the belt to hold up the trousers. Danny investigated. It was some kind of purse; in it were six coins. What were they worth? Danny had no idea. With the doublet on, the pouch was hidden from view. Now I've got two bags round my waist, he thought.

Besides the clothes, there were two rather small, reddish-brown apples on the block. He picked them up and was just about to take a bite out of one, when something flashed in his brain – 'don't eat anything' it went. Danny couldn't remember a SHARP commandment to that effect but perhaps it was best to be careful, just in case. Then he heard a soft whinnying noise. Of course, the apples are for the horse. He went up to the grey and stroked its nose. It tossed its head and then nuzzled his cheek and shoulder. I seem to be very popular with animals in the olden times, he thought, remembering the little spaniel, Beauty.

"Steady on, old fellow, you'll biff me over at this rate. You know I've got something for you, don't you?" Danny held out an apple on the flat of his hand and the animal's big floppy lips closed softly around it. The horse poked its head forward and, in what seemed like horse ecstasy, crunched it between its flat yellow teeth. A dribble of juice escaped down one side of its lower jaw. Danny waited until the horse had savoured the last remaining apple moment and then offered the second one.

As he gave the horse a final pat and turned away from the stable, Danny heard a commotion and three lads came laughing and careering into the yard. Of course, he thought, remembering the instruction: 'Wait at your landing spot until someone comes to collect you.'

"We knew you'd be hiding here Tobias, old chap," one of them shouted as if he had said something very clever. "Trying to give us the slip, eh? Though it's not us you'll want to give the slip but that scoundrel Edward Rode, no doubt."

"Why ever should I want to do that?" replied Danny, judging that his response might give him some idea of what was going on, and if not it could be taken as a joke – which it was.

The three slapped their thighs and rolled about laughing so much, Danny thought he was going to be none the wiser, but then one chap sobered up enough to speak.

"That's a good'un master Toby. When there's not been a word spoken in the hall for the last three days but about the challenge you gave Edward Rode last Sunday in church. Why there's been more wagers laid, more than ever there was for William, your brother. But then it was a done thing that William would beat Richard Rode. I mean no contest, nor there was really. But with you…" There were more outbursts of laughter, this time a bit sheepish from the other two and one lad pointed his finger at the other and said:

"And some amongst us, naming no names, has been a traitor." Clearly he didn't need to name names as he was pointing directly at the other lad who went a bright red colour.

"Well, I haven't got money to spare like you two, have I?" said the 'traitor' who was the largest and roughest looking of the three.

"Aye, but Hugh, betting against your own!" The first lad, who seemed to be the leader, was looking cross now and the laughing had stopped. There was an uncomfortable silence.

"You mean, I might lose?" Danny asked, thinking it was best to bring as much out into the open as possible, but not knowing what on earth it was he was going to lose.

"Not might, almost definitely will," the 'traitor' was sticking to his guns.

"That's no way to talk, Hugh Smethers," said the first lad who was clearly getting angry, and he gave the burly lad a push.

"I'll say what I think, you dolt head. Who are you, Samuel Bates to be telling me what to say? All but a fool would back Tobias against Edward. Oh I grant you, Tobias will no doubt win the chess tonight at the board, but that's it. Every other contest, including the horse race, even given that Apple here is a fast horse, Tobias Moreton will lose – and as for the swim! I think he'll drown himself halfway across the pond, so let's hope that swimming comes out last in the draw, else there'll be no challenge for folk to gawp at. And since when could Tobias kick a ball? He'll not shift it up the field more that a few hand widths, never mind get it between them two posts, and from all I've heard tell, Edward Rode is a fast runner…" he spread his hands out as if to say, no further explanation needed. Clearly Tobias's reputation as a runner was as bad as his reputation in all other sporting events.

Depressingly, Danny could see that the other two, despite them having been his supporters a few minutes before, were now nodding their heads in agreement – there was a very noticeable lack of hilarity.

It looks, thought Danny, as if Tobias has got himself into some kind of a mess. He's no sportsman but he has challenged another guy to what looks like nothing short of a decathlon. The thing was, that now he was Tobias, he was the decathlon contender. The thought crept into his mind: perhaps he could do better than Tobias. Danny was beginning to feel an extraordinary tingle of excitement. It was the feeling he got when Mark passed him the ball and he had ran with it until there was only the goalie in front of him - his skill against the goalie's. Brilliant. And what about that time he ran in the 100 metres against Blakey, the fastest runner in Year 6? But he had beaten him, against the odds he had beaten him. He had loved that feeling of coming in front of Blakey by an inch. Not that he could do it again. Blakey ran for the Harriers now. The point was, he had done it then.

"Look, you three. Cheer up will you? I'm going to do my best, and a chap can't do more than that can he?" They all three looked at him and there were mutters of 'well said Tobias' even from the surly Hugh. Then the one who seemed to be the leader, came over and gave him a friendly thump on the back.

"We know you will try your best Tobias, but the truth is we know it won't be enough. You can back out now, you know. Just because your grandfather started the stupid feud between the Moretons and the Rodes, it doesn't mean you've got to carry it on."

"Aye, but how would it look, Samuel, if a Moreton lad turned thirteen didn't challenge a Rode?"

"Well Edward Rode turned his fourteenth year last quarter and that's not rightly fair."

Oh, so I'm supposed to be thirteen and I'm up against a fourteen-year-old and I've not yet turned twelve. Definitely, this is not fair, thought Danny. He could get out of it, he supposed. Dash out of the yard and hide somewhere and press the emergency button to go back. But there was no way. He was feeling more and more psyched up about the prospect of going against Edward Rhode. Almost as if he knew him, he wanted to beat him. Edward Rode must be a loud-mouthed bully, of that he was sure or why else would the weedy, chess-playing Tobias have challenged him?

Danny turned round towards the grey, who was

still straining at the stable gate. "Have you been listening to all this, Apple?" he asked "We've got to win, even though Hugh here thinks we'll lose." The horse whinnied and tossed its head.

"Well if you're set on carrying it through, Tobias, we had better get a move on. They're waiting for you in the home meadow. Edward's been there a while now and there's a right gathering. All work's stopped for this."

"Had we better bring Apple with us?" asked the quiet one of the three.

"No James, if it's the horse race first, it will be up to the Marl pit, setting off at the top path, and you can dodge in and get Apple for master Tobias then."

As Danny and his new friends approached the home meadow, the noisy hurly-burly from the men, women and children that were gathered there quietened down. Talk stopped and people moved aside to let them through to the inner circle, where a sturdy young man with thick dark hair and not so much as a smile on his scowling face, called out as soon as he spotted Danny:

"So, Tobias Moreton, you've decided to show, have you? I thought you might have got your sister,

Mary to stand in for you." There were roars of laughter from his supporters at this and cries of "Shame!" from those that must have been Moreton supporters.

Danny felt his face go bright red, and anger, such as he had never felt before, seemed to surge through his body. He clenched his fists.

"Steady on Tobias," Samuel muttered at his side.

"You had best keep your jeering till you have won," shouted back Danny.

"Aye, well that won't be long then will it? You know that even if you win the straw, you can't start with the chess. That can only take place after nightfall."

"Aye, I know that," said Danny, not knowing at all. Then he became aware that everyone was looking towards a tall grey-haired man wearing a long robe tied with a simple knotted cord, a man of the church. He was holding out his two fists and a thin brown stalk protruded from each. Was there some etiquette to observe, Danny wondered? But he did not need to wonder for long. Edward Rode strode forward saying:

"As a visitor on Moreton land, I shall draw first." He pulled out the straw from the clergyman's right hand. As he held it aloft there was an "ahhhh," from the crowd, some looking jubilant, others downcast.

Danny went forward and pulled his straw. It was easy to see that it was the shorter of the two.

"As adjudicator, I must ask you, Edward Rode, in what area of endeavour do you choose to first challenge master Tobias Moreton."

"I challenge Tobias Moreton to swim across the Mill Pond as many times as he can without putting his foot to soil and if I am still swimming, when he can swim no further, I shall be declared the winner."

The three lads standing beside him groaned. Danny noticed that even Hugh, who had placed a bet that Edward Rode would win, looked sorry.

"Well Hugh, isn't that what you wanted?" he couldn't resist asking. Hugh shrugged and said:

"Don't bear it against me, Tobias. It was only the money. I'm a Moreton supporter through and through."

"Well, I've not lost yet." Danny said. But now he was not worrying about how long he could swim for; he had, after all, got a quantity of medals for long-distance swimming. What he was worrying about, was how on earth he was going to get into the water? Did these people swim in their clothes? If so, he wouldn't get far. Did they perhaps take off all their clothes? Surely not? —not with women around. One thing was for certain, no one had Lycra trunks like the ones in his bedroom drawer.

CHAPTER 8

A Swim In The Mill Pond

Fortunately, Edward Rode had set off first, lead-ing the crowd down a track through the grass, towards the mill pond. I'll just have to copy what he does, Danny surmised. But if it is swimming in the buff, peo-ple will notice the strange bag stuck to my tummy!

As they strode along, Samuel issued a stream of instructions, telling Tobias to swim slowly and not to waste his energies on trying to go fast. The other two kept chipping in, reminding him that the race would be won, not by how many times across the pond he swam, but how long he kept his head above water.

"Old man Hadleigh and his son have a boat or two out on the pond so that if a chap should start going under they can row over and fish him out." Samuel said to console him.

"So glad to hear that," said Danny, his sarcasm lost on his companions. All the while, various ones from old men and women to rosy-cheeked kids, wished him luck and patted him on the back. He could tell that it was a real day out for them and suddenly the weather joined in. It had been rather overcast and cloudy up until then, but the clouds were scattering and soon a bright, early summer's sun was warming them up.

Up until this point, Danny had not thought about his location. *I should recognise where I am,* he thought. *Kaz had said you only went back to somewhere you had been before, but I don't remember this place at all.* He turned around to look back the way they had come. Not far off, across the rolling grass was a large house made of wooden beams and grey plaster, not as grand or as extensive as Bramall, but of a similar construction. Danny could see though, that it had no glass in its windows and that along one side, it was covered in poles and planks of wood, as if building work was in progress. *Perhaps,* he thought *that is why I don't recognise it, perhaps it's not finished?* Still, his mind roved back over the places he had visited with the family in the last couple of years. He sighed, there had been so many of them and, of course, he never usually paid much attention. Samuel pulled at his sleeve, obviously interpreting his backward stare with another meaning.

"Your sister Mary is sure to come – she won't stay cross with you all day. You had best not dawdle too much Tobias, or that fellow will be crowing again."

By the time they arrived at the place chosen for the start of the swim, most of the women had settled themselves on the bank of the wide pond, with the smaller children tucked in beside them, and the older ones excitedly jumping up and down, or running about changing places, unable to decide on the best vantage point. The men stood together in a solid and more sober group. Most of the bank was bordered by reeds and rushes but here there was an indentation and a small sloping beach of muddy sand. A soft breeze was rippling the surface and a few yards out, a small rowing boat was moored.

As Danny had hoped, Edward Rode, surrounded by his supporters, was well ahead with his preparations for his swim. He had taken off most of his clothes, but not his shirt. He was busy tying the two ends of the shirt together under his legs. Ah, I see, we swim in our shirts, thought Danny relieved. He hurriedly took off his clothes and copied what Edward had done with the shirt. He was glad to find that he could easily tie the shirt between his legs so no danger of his modern underpants or the time/space bag showing.

"Remember, touch the prow of the boat as soon as you can and turn round to swim back again, both sides," said Samuel, helpful as always but not realising, of course, just how much Danny needed this information.

Edward Rode was grinning now, mocking Tobias without saying a word. His grinning made the angry feeling come back. Danny felt his throat tighten, but he said nothing. Edward strode into the gently rippling water. After a few steps, the water was above his knees and he bent down, cupped his hands and splashed water onto the thick muscles of his upper arm.

"Good Luck," Samuel gave Danny a gentle push forward. Danny walked in, feeling the soft muddy sand under his toes. The water was cold. Danny shivered. He wanted to plunge in, but Edward Rode was still splashing himself, so Danny copied him. Then Edward walked forward until the water was almost up to his chin. Danny was level with him. About ten metres out from the shore, Edward turned to hiss:

"No one knows how deep it gets, but when you're out there you won't be able to touch the bottom and when it closes over your daft head, you'll drown." He started swimming.

"And the best of luck to you too, you miserable git!" Even though his anger made him want to strike out with his fast, well-practised front crawl, Danny waited and watched, only starting to swim properly when Edward was about five metres in front. Edward's head bobbed above the water, but Danny couldn't tell what stroke he was doing. One arm seemed to come out every other stroke but he certainly wasn't doing a front crawl and it didn't look like the breast stroke. He was going at about the speed of the 'slow lane' plodders at the baths. Danny and his mum always powered up and down the fast lane and even Jenny had been promoted to the middle lane. All the way across, Danny cruised behind Edward, using the breast stroke. Sometimes he had to tread water so as not to catch him up. Every now and again he checked that his phone was still in place, thankful that its properties included being completely indestructible and completely waterproof.

On the other side of the mill pond, there was a small group of people watching to see that there was no cheating.

"No foot to the ground," they yelled.

A small boat bobbed at anchor about five metres out from the shore. Edward touched it and turned. As he passed Danny on the way in, he tried another of his mocking grins but with the water slapping into his face it didn't come off very well. And so they swam back over to the other side. As they reached the home shore, cheering voices came drifting over the surface of the water:

"Keep it up Toby!"

"Hurrah for Edward!"

"Swim strong! Swim steady!" Well it's steady alright thought Danny.

They turned at the marker boat and started swimming back across, Danny still keeping Edward several metres in front of him. So it went for another two crossings. Danny had settled into one of those slow rhythms that good swimmers can keep up, seemingly indefinitely, arms, legs synchronised, mind almost blank. But then on the next turn, he looked at Edward and saw he was struggling. He was splashing a lot and slowing down considerably.

A nasty thought came. Edward was not the giving up type. He had thought that Tobias would be easily beaten and now he has almost reached his limit, but he was not going to give up. That chap is going to keep going, come what may. Suppose he goes down in the middle of the pond? Danny wondered what on earth would he do. He would have to try and save him and that would be difficult and also not at all what Tobias Moreton would be able to do.

Suddenly Danny increased his pace and came to within a foot or so of the struggling Edward, who by this time was far too desperate keeping his head above water to notice what his opponent was doing. Danny took a deep breath and dived down under the surface. He swam forward until in the murky water he could see Edward's trailing legs. He grasped Edward's ankle, giving it a hefty tug. Edward kicked out and Danny bobbed up to the surface in time to hear Edward's anguished screams:

Splashing as if in trouble himself, Danny shouted: "What is it Edward?"

"Som't tried to drag me down." He gasped for breath and spluttered out mouthfuls of water. "There's som't evil in this pond."

"Aye, I felt it too. We must swim together to ward it off!"

Danny swam alongside the struggling Edward, willing him to get to the bank. At one point, Edward's head disappeared below the surface, but after an agonising moment he came up again. He's a fighter, I'll give him that, thought Danny, and now for sure he is fighting for his life. He's like a waterlogged dinghy, just keeping above the surface, ready to go down at any minute. Inch by inch, it seemed to Danny, they got nearer to the home bank. Now the prow of the marker boat was only a few feet off and this seemed to give Edward encouragement. Making a last effort, he gave a spurt forward. His arm came out and he struck the water with determination. Stretching out a hand he grabbed the mooring rope. Danny sighed with relief and trod water. Edward gasped in air, choking, spluttering and holding on to the rope for dear life.

"There's something out there, something evil waiting to drag a man down. We can't swim on. You agree?" Edward was done for, but still he did not want to face the possibility of being beaten by Tobias. Danny so much wanted to beat Edward – to swim back over to the other side, but he knew if he turned around the stupid Edward might try to follow. He would have to settle for a draw.

"It's a draw Edward." Danny conceded. Then he heard to his amazement:

"Oh no it ain't ," Edward was gaining a little of his former bluster now that he was hanging on to the rope. "I swam ahead of you, so I should be counted the winner." Danny couldn't believe his ears. But he was wary, he mustn't challenge him.

"Oh all right. You did swim faster. You're the winner."

At these words, Edward tried to give one of his mocking grins but he was choking too much with a belly full of water. He pushed himself towards the shore. His feet touched ground and he started wading out. Then he heard a great cheer go up from the crowd. Danny, not having touched the rope or put a foot to the ground had spun round and was swimming back out across to the other side. All Edward could do was watch in dismay.

Hugh, Samuel and James were beside themselves. They raced round the mill pond to meet him as he pulled himself out on the far bank, the undisputed winner. Someone wrapped a huge sheepskin round the shivering Danny and the three lads fell on him with 'Hurrahs' and 'Well done's' and so many little friendly punches and hugs that Danny was bowled over on to the soft grass and all four of them fell about laughing. James had brought Danny's clothes and this included a dry shirt. Danny got dressed quickly, keen to make sure that no one could spot the phone bag stuck to his stomach.

Then they set off back to the home field, still in high spirits, Samuel giving a commentary re-run of the swim. He had spotted that Danny's head had gone below the water just before Edward had got into trouble on the last leg back, but he had assumed that was because he was in trouble as well.

"My goodness Tobias, we had such a fright. We thought you were done for, drowning at the bottom of the mill pond."

"Well, I came up again didn't I?"

"Aye and went on to swim another length," crowed James.

They were so happy, sharing that wonderful feeling of victory over a hated enemy and Danny felt as if he had known Samuel, Hugh and James all his life.

CHAPTER 9

The Lead Balloon

When they got back to the home field, the crowd had become very jolly; people were laughing, joking, eating and drinking. Wooden boards had been placed on barrels to make tables and dotted about were large sacks filled with straw for people to sit on. Jugs and flagons of drink were placed on the makeshift tables.

A girl, holding three tankards in one hand and two in another, came towards Danny and the lads. Hugh joked with her as he took the tankards from her and passed them in turn to each of them, making sure that Danny was given the first one. Forgetting his concerns about whether he should eat and drink, Danny took a sip and then a huge gulp. It was a weak beer and tasted good. When James, the eager gofer, came back with some rough, flat cakes, spread thickly with honey, Danny tucked in with the rest of them. After all that swimming, he was starving.

They settled down on a couple of squashy sacks, not caring about the spikes of straw that poked through the sack and through their woollen hose. Suddenly, Samuel scrambled to his feet followed by the other two. Danny looked up and saw a man and woman coming towards them. They looked important personages, dressed more finely than others. You could tell that people treated them with deference, making way for them as they passed by, and some showing respect with a small bow. The woman held tightly onto the man's arm.

"You father approaches Tobias," said Samuel in a low voice. Danny scrambled to his feet just as the man and woman stopped in front of them.

"The Lord be praised! You have done us proud, so far, Tobias. Let's hope you can keep it up." The man shook Tobias's hand. His looks were stern but the woman beside him was full of smiles.

"Well, done, well done, my Tobias." Once again Danny found himself crushed against the bosom of a woman from four centuries before his birth. This time, the discomfort lasted a little longer; the rosy cheeked woman ruffled his hair and held him so tightly he could feel the straight-lacing of her bodice against his cheek. When she let him go, the couple turned and walked away to join a group of older people standing with the clergyman. Danny's friends grinned at him as if to say, trust parents to be a pain, and then they all collapsed down again on the squashy sacks. James gathered up their empty tankards and went to one of the tables for a refill.

"You know what," said Samuel, "Tobias should be down there with the lads kicking the ball, getting the feel of it."

"That's right; he should," said Hugh. "But what about the choice of contest Tobias? As the winner you have the right to the next choice. Which will you go for? The running, striking the ball or the horse race?"

"I'm not sure yet. What would you pick?"

"Edward Rode can kick that ball to the next village," said Samuel.

"Aye, he can," agreed Hugh. "Maybe you'd be best going for the run, Tobias —now you've rattled him a bit with the swimming, but then…"

"But then what ?" Danny asked.

"Well, I don't remember you being so good at running Tobias but that's what I thought with the swimming. I think you've been practising on the quiet, and good on you, that's all I can say."

"Yes well. You know what? I've something on my mind." Danny paused and the other two looked at him. "I've been worrying about your bet Hugh." Hugh shifted about uncomfortably and then muttered:

"That's not for you to worry about, Master Tobias."

"Aye, it is Hugh. As you say, I've been practising on the quiet and I should have let my friends know." Hugh didn't speak.

"How much did you lay out?" Again Hugh didn't answer. Samuel was listening. He was not joining in but he was looking very serious. Danny couldn't tell what he was thinking. Danny took out the six coins that were in the bag at his waist. "Was it this much?" He opened his hand with the coins in his palm.

"Course not. I've not got that sort of money, have I?"

"Well, I want you to take this and if I win, I want you to take out the amount you have lost."

"What are you saying Tobias?" exclaimed Samuel. "Why should you do that? If you really want to give this fool his money back, you can do so after you've won. Honestly Tobias you always were a soft-'un."

"Look, Samuel, I really want Hugh to take these coins from me now. You never know what might happen, and I will feel so much better going out against Edward, if I know that Hugh here is not going to suffer by my winning."

"Like I say, you always were a soft'un," Samuel said. He didn't agree but he wasn't going to argue.

"Like I said, you just don't know what might happen."

James, who by now had returned with the filled tankards and was wondering why no one was relieving him of the slurping beers, chipped in with:

"That's right – Tobias could fall from Apple when he jumps the ditch and crack his head open on a boulder." This comment brought howls from Hugh and Samuel. They jumped up and started telling James off for such a stupid remark and teasing him about his own poor riding skills. Just the same, they took the tankards from him and started downing the contents. While they were drinking Danny quietly pressed the six coins into Hugh's hand.

Then they set off through the crowd to join a noisy group of lads and men chasing after a brown muddy ball. Danny got a touch or two. Crikey, he thought. Talk about a 'lead balloon'! There was no rise in it at all. It just bumped across the ground, or rolled whenever there was a bit of a downward slope.

Suddenly, one of the older men held up his hand and, at great risk of being bashed in the head, stooped down to pick up the ball. He pointed up the field to where the old man from the church had got up on a wooden bench and was waving his arms as if to call people round. The men near Danny propelled him forward until he was standing within a few feet of the clergyman. Edward Rode was there next to him.

"Tobias Moreton. You were the winner of the first contest," called out the old man in a surprisingly strong firm voice. "What is your choice for the second?"

"Striking the football, Sir."

Two men busily hammered a couple of stakes into the ground roughly the distance apart of two goal posts, and a rope was laid on the ground about twenty yards away from the posts. The ball was placed just a foot or so the other side of the rope. Impromptu stewards marshalled people to the sidelines. Danny and Edward took up positions behind the rope. Edward started to hop from foot to foot and jump up and down. Just like a premier league footballer about to take a penalty, thought Danny.

There was a toss of a coin to decide who went first, and much to Danny's relief, Edward won the toss. As Edward strode forward to kick the ball, there was determination in every inch of him. He brought his foot back and thud, he sent the ball over the grass at a pretty good pace – a good kick. The crowd let out a cheer, but then there were cries of:

"Oh no!" and "bad luck Edward!"

The ball skimmed past one of the posts, just inches on the wrong side. Two small boys chased after it and fought each other to be the one to run back with it to the next contestant.

Danny's turn to kick. He squinted down the track. With a proper ball he would have no difficulty placing it between those two posts and sending it on way further. But with this ball, he had no idea how he would do. He took his time, and then struck it straight and true through the posts, but it felt as if he had just kicked a rock. He limped back across the line. When the ball stopped rolling, a man pushed a stick into the ground to show where it had reached.

Edward's turn again. This time he took even more care, eyeing the space between the posts, and swinging his foot back several times, before striking the ball with a hefty thud. Something about Edward's strong powerful shoulders and the set of his head as he leant back to deliver a scorching kick reminded Danny of Wayne Rooney. Wow, that was a fantastic kick! It shot on past Danny's stick by about ten yards!

As Edward walked back, Danny called out,

"Well done Edward!" Edward looked really surprised and then muttered a gruff 'thank you'.

As it turned out, that was the winning kick.

Danny had no idea how many attempts they would each have but just kept trying his best. Danny's next two balls were short of his first, but his fifth amazingly rolled on to only about a hand span behind Edward's winner. Edward's other tries never matched his second shot.

After Danny's fifth kick, the spry old clergyman galloped over to them, his long robe swishing round his ankles and the wooden cross on his chest bouncing up and down in time with his feet. He raised Edward's arm to show the winner. There was much cheering from the crowd. Danny joined in. Edward turned to him and for the first time said a friendly word.

"Your aim was true and good Tobias Moreton, I'll give you that." They shook hands and the crowd cheered. Danny thought: that's the magic of football.

CHAPTER 10

Run For Your Life Danny

Edward chose the run next and it seemed that there was to be little let up between the two contests. Two men pulled up the two football posts and took them to the edge of the field. They were then hammered in, along with others so as to make a circular track. All the spectators were herded into the middle and Danny and Edward were ushered to a starting point, once again marked by the rope.

Danny looked around desperately for Samuel, Hugh or James. There were crowds of people milling about, but he couldn't spot his friends. He didn't want to start the race not knowing its length. Edward's mates had brought him more to eat; he was chewing on a chicken leg and swilling down a tankard of ale. The clergyman was ready to start the race, and Danny would have had to go without the information he wanted, if it were not for a quantity of small children, who had decided they were going to have a go at racing themselves. Despite the best efforts of their mothers and sisters, some were scampering along at top speed down the track, while others were making practice starts at the line. The clergyman shook his head with annoyance and wagged a finger at them but they took no notice.

"Get those children off the course!" he bellowed.

Danny spotted Samuel coming towards him, carrying a tankard.

"We thought you might need a drink before the race, but that greedy lot up there had finished the barrel off and it was a while before a new one came."

"Thanks." Danny took a couple of gulps. "What I can't remember Samuel, is how long the race is." At this, Samuel looked at him strangely.

"Why three times round the field, as always. But what difference the length of a race Tobias? You just need to run as fast as you can until the end." Danny said nothing. Thinking of the tactics used by modern runners, he was already planning his strategy.

"Runners take your place," called the clergyman and a hush descended on the gathering.

"Go!" A single word and the two runners were away, Edward setting a cracking pace, just as Danny thought he would. Danny let Edward get five yards in front of him and kept it like that all the way round the first circuit and half way through the second. As the third circuit started, Edward's pace began to slacken. Danny crept up on him but kept him just in front. He could hear cries of:

"Come on Tobias!"

"Catch him Tobias!"

"Speed up Tobias!" And as he pounded round, he could see the stern face of the tall man, Tobias's father and the fearful face of the woman beside him, watching the race through the fingers of her hands. Samuel, Hugh and James waved him on at several points, obviously careering across the grass to pick him up on the other side. He knew that they thought he was losing, unable to pass Edward. But now, even though he was still several paces behind, Danny was sure he could beat Edward.

On the second from final bend of the last circuit, he closed the gap. Edward was a one pace runner, but Danny had another gear to go up. At this point, the phone began to vibrate. It hardly registered with him. All he could think of was quickening his stride and passing Edward. The finishing line was ten yards off. Danny drew level. Five yards off, he went past Edward as if he were standing still, feet pounding the turf, arms pumping the air, the cheers of the crowd in his ears. He lifted his arms as he crossed the rope. Although his blood was thumping in his head, he heard the old man cry:

"Tobias Moreton the winner!"

Still the phone was vibrating. A crowd of people gathered round him, exclaiming, patting him on the back. A pretty girl came and kissed him on the cheek and said:

"Your sister Mary is very proud of you."

His phone was still vibrating – and now it entered Danny's consciousness. Gasping for breath, longing to throw himself on the ground, he dodged under arms, weaved through groups and ran, ran out of the home field up the track towards the barn. But someone was on his heels. He glanced behind him – it was Samuel.

Danny stopped and turned round. "Please Samuel! Please help me. I've got to go and see Apple and I need to go alone." Danny bent double. He had the most awful stitch in his side. Still the phone was vibrating.

"Tobias, whatever is it? You look as if you have seen a ghost."

Ah ghost, that's it, these people really believe in ghosts. "When I was running round the track, I got the most dreadful feeling that something was up with

Apple, something not natural." Still panting heavily, Danny struggled to get the words out. "There's been some really strange things happening today, ghostly things. Please be the best of friends and go back to the home field. I'll be down again in a minute, you see."

Samuel looked amazed at Danny's stricken face. "Is it...is it something evil? Edward's been giving out that there was something unspeakable in the mill pond."

"Something like that. Please Samuel, go back."

"If that's what you want Tobias, of course I will." Samuel was a true friend. He didn't question any further but turned and walked back down the path.

Fear drove Danny to run the last few yards to the barns. Just as he turned in through the rickety gate, the phone stopped vibrating. For a second, Danny froze. Then he dashed to Apple's stable, opened the door and let the horse out. He shut the door behind him and, with trembling fingers, took off his clothes, leaving them in a pile in one corner of the stable. Was he too late? Would he still be able to leave even if the phone had stopped vibrating? He didn't know.

He prayed that he was going to get back home. Then dialled 15978 and pressed the red button. Nothing. He was still standing in his underpants in a horse's stable! Panic was gripping every inch of him. He dialled 15978 again. Nothing. He dialled again. He peered at the phone. In the darkness of the stable, it was impossible to see the screen. He stepped outside. He was now shaking from head to toe and it was as much as he could do to lift the phone and look at it.

The words 'Number not recognised' were displayed. Number not recognised? Slowly the thought entered his head – he had mis-dialled. What had he dialled? The sound of voices came near. People were just about to come into the yard. Then Apple trotted forward, swishing her tail. She headed out of the gate and around the corner, straight into whoever was approaching. Danny heard cries of:

"Apple's loose!" The sound of the horse's hooves clattered more loudly as if she had broken into a fast trot. There were noises of a chase, people trying to grab Apple's halter. Voices getting further away, as the capture of the horse became a priority.

Danny steadied himself. Then he slowly recited 1-5-7-9-8. He dialled that number and pressed the red button. A faint high-pitched whine pierced the air.

That evening, Danny ate an enormous helping of vegetable pie (another of Mrs. Higgins's tasty but often-served meals). He nursed a stitch and wondered how long it would take for the bruise on his big toe to stop hurting. He also wondered if Tobias won the race on Apple and he thought that even if he didn't, Tobias would go into the last contest two all, and everyone was sure he would beat Edward at chess, so he would be the ultimate winner. But then, upsets to even a sure thing could happen and, after all, it was only a friendly match.

Just before he drifted off to sleep, Danny murmured: "Thanks Apple. You were the one that got me back home – I wish I had got to ride you."

Danny did not have to wait long for a message from SHARP. The next day, he heard the familiar and distinctive pulsing buzz that came from either his phone or his computer when SHARP was sending a message. He went over to his computer and there was the introductory blue screen, followed by a short message from Kaz:

Thank you Danny for a very successful trip. Am I right in thinking you've not suffered with time slip as badly as last time?

Danny typed back: It's been tons better this time. I felt a bit peculiar this morning but I concentrated hard on my immediate surroundings, even noticing the burnt toast smell from Mum in the kitchen, and it worked as you said it would. I did just the same when I was in 1588 in the farm-yard, only there I had to concentrate on a disgusting smell of manure.

Good.

Just a one word reply.

By the way, where was I? I can't remember having gone anywhere like that with my family. Danny typed.

You were in Little Moreton Hall in Cheshire. I'm

sorry but I've got to go now, Danny. I'll be back in touch soon, I hope. There's some big problems and I'm about to lose transm....

The screen went blank. Danny stared at the empty screen, unable to comprehend that there could be problems for the all-powerful SHARP. He wondered what was causing it – probably a minor technical fault. Perhaps their servers were down? He grinned to himself, knowing it could be nothing like that. But, what a good job it had happened after he got back to 2008!

He read and re-read Kaz's message, getting anxious as the minutes slipped by. After waiting for more than an hour to see if another message came through, he got up and went downstairs to find his mum.

"When did we go to Little Moreton Hall, Mum?"

"Errr – it's two or maybe three years ago. A wonderful example of a timber-framed manor house from the Tudor period, possibly the best in the country. Don't you remember it? It had that strange long gallery on the top floor. You and Jenny wanted to race up and down it, and some woman who was very knowledgeable about the place, said that was probably what small children in Tudor times actually did, when no important ladies were about, of course."

"Oh, the place where you were right at the top of the house and the floor boards sloped down so you didn't really feel safe up there."

"That's right – the top storey, making up the gallery, was added in a very cowboy fashion, and the National Trust have had to do some very extensive work under-pinning it."

"But there wasn't a lake or pond there!" Danny's unguarded exclamation, slipped out without his thinking.

"Well no. Why did you think there should be?"

"Errr well, I don't know – it's just that big halls often do have lakes and stuff." Danny tried to sound vague to cover up. Mrs Higgins looked puzzled but didn't ask any more questions.

"It's strange you should have said that, because for many years there were two large stretches of water at Little Moreton. One was the millpond and the other was almost a lake called the Marl. It served an extremely old iro-foundry called a bloomery." Mrs Higgins walked over to a shelf where she kept all the guide books for the places they visited. "Look you can read about them in here Danny."

Danny took the book and went upstairs. There in

the visitors' guide, he found a map showing where the millpond used to be, now only visible as a dip in the grassland on aerial photographs.

For days Danny waited to hear from SHARP again. The days turned into weeks and then into months and still there was no contact from Kaz or anyone else from the future. Danny began to believe that it was over – no more time travel. He felt as if he'd been grounded.

He missed the excitement of it, but he kept himself busy, writing about his two adventures and posting them on his website. He tried to draw pictures to illustrate the stories but try as he could, even though he was good at illustrations, he could not draw the things he had seen on his adventures into the past. It was as if the people's faces so clear in his memory would not transpose themselves to paper. He even tried to make up an adventure of his own using his mother's guidebooks for information, but his heart wasn't in it. Deep down inside he believed that Kaz would get back in touch again. He was right but it was a long wait.

Competitions And Activities

Mark Christie of Stockport was
the winner of our 2010 book
illustration competition with this
drawing of Danny wearing
the clothes of a boy in
1615.
The competition
judge, the teacher at
Bramall Hall, chose this
illustration because she
liked the simplicity of
the pencil line and she
thought it looked like
a 21st century boy in
17th century clothing.
Maybe you can be a
winner next time.
Watch our website

www.sevenarchespublishing.co.uk for the next
opportunity to show us what a good illustrator you
are.

Publishing With Principles

Our books for children are not only exciting adventures, they stretch and challenge them as readers and learners, and are unlikely to pander to the latest trends. Our first book, 'Nidae's Promise' encouraged wonder at the amazing life of swallows. Danny Higgins – Time Traveller, the first in our series 'The Time-Travelling Kids' celebrates the history of our nation.

We are striving to make our business a good place for people to work and to offer employment to those, who through disabilities or other reasons, have found it difficult to get work elsewhere.

Our books are printed in this country so that delivery is nearby and the paper used is from managed forests.

Contact Us

You are welcome to contact Seven Arches Publishing by:

Phone: 0161 4257642

Or

Email: admin@sevenarchespublishing.co.uk

Acknowledgements

The writer gained knowledge of, and enthusiasm for, both Bramall Hall and Little Moreton Hall from her frequent visits to these lovely timber-framed manor houses. The book 'Bramall Hall The Story of an Elizabethan Manor House' by E. Barbara Dean was an indispensable source of information for Danny's adventure back in time to this Cheshire manor house. The National Trust guidebook inspired Danny's adventure at Little Moreton Hall.

Collect the next books in the Time Traveller Kids series

Danny has become an experienced Time traveller but this doesn't help him when SHARP's systems fail and he is left stranded in 671 when wolves roamed the English country-side.

Incredibly musically gifted, Atlanta is entranced by the music of the far-into-the- future humankind. Is this what makes her agree to join the growing band of twenty first century kids who go back in time to gather information, for the organisation called SHARP?

When Alex McLean is catapulted back to 1314 by a rival outfit to SHARP, his life is in serious danger. They do not care if he falls to his death with the desperate band of Scots fighters who did the impossible and scaled the terrifying Rock on which Edinburgh Castle stands to this day.